THE GATE KEEPER

CONSUMMATION BY LIGHT

ANTHONY JOHN HOARE

Authorunit
17130 Van Buren Blvd., Ste. 238,
Riverside, CA 92504
877-826-5888
www.authorunit.com

ISBN 979-8-89030-014-0 (Paperback)
ISBN 979-8-89030-015-7 (Ebook)
ISBN 979-8-89030-096-6 (hardcover)

Printed in the United States of America

CONTENTS

CHAPTER 1

The archeological site was unusually lonely for this time of the day. Being consumed in work had diminished the perception of her surroundings and making her totally indifferent to the fact she'd been left alone. The team had finished early for the day and had probably made their way back down the base camp trail. Focused on her assigned project, she was completely unaware it was well past the time she'd planned on quitting. Time seemed immaterial because of the importance she'd placed on the success of this assignment. Her need to impress Joe, team leader and father figure, was paramount at this stage of her career. Having forgotten to pack her knee pads, she continued to meticulously remove the top cover from what she perceived to be a significant find with sore knees.

"Hello Ruth, I'd have expected you to have finished this by now." She looked up into the face of a young man with strikingly distinctive features. She did not perceive him as being overly handsome, yet his smile seemed to possess a gentle understanding quality that captivated her.

"Excuse me! Who are you? Where did you come from?" This archeological team was a small, close-knit family. So, who was this stranger? This was an isolated mountainous area with limited access in or out. Half-hour hike from base camp and days from civilization. How had this person looking down at her arrived unannounced? The arrival of a new team member would have been a hot topic of conversation, and there had been none. She did not feel threatened but instead strangely comforted by his presence.

"Of course, you know me. I told you to call me Peter, then you nicknamed me 'Peter, Peter the pearly gates keeper' for a short time, which you later shortened to Perter Gates. You don't seem to have the capacity at present to recall our past encounters." A devilish smile lit up his face as he made this somewhat demeaning comment. He pointed to a doorway to nowhere carved into the rock face. "I came from there."

"You're talking in riddles. That makes no sense whatsoever. You must have come from the base camp. Why didn't one of the team accompany you back here?"

"As I explained, I came from there." A grin lit up his face as he again pointed vigorously in a prodding manner at the rock face with the doorway to nowhere.

"You're talking foolishly and still making no sense."

"Then I will have to convince you. Come." He held out his hand in a gesture of assistance. She accepted the invitation with her own hand. "And bring that artifact with you." Withdrawing her hand, she slowly lifted the tablet that had been so meticulously unearthed from her dig. He walked her towards the portal. "There are some basic things I need to explain before we proceed further." She knew this was going to be some con job, but at the same time, she was intrigued by his sales pitch. "First off, do you believe in Heaven?"

"That's an odd question; let's say yes to keep it simple."

"Oh, I like simple. Well, let's say heaven is a universe composed predominantly of light-matter. Our universe consists mostly of dark matter, for want of a better word. Predominantly, our skies are black. Only stars light up the heavens in our universe: In contrast, the universe of light contains abundant incandescent material with dark spots filling the sky, much like the stars here. This incandescent material is the substance stars require to burn. Without light, there is no fire."

"Are you going to bullshit me with some cockamamie theory about dark matter?" He gave a chuckle

"Well, now you've brought that subject up, let me put it in layman's terms. First, I like to pose a question? Where does the light go when it extinguishes? Please allow me to provide that answer. It's replaced by dark. Light passes through the vial into the universe of light, and the universe of light expels the same amount of dark back through the veil to compensate. One element, light, pushes while the other dark element pulls. This keeps the perfect balance of yin and yang between the two universes. You see dark travels at the same speed as light. That's how it can immediately replace the light. This portal is part of a machine that enables us to ride those constant cosmic tides as they flow to and fro. Under normal circumstances, only your spirit, ghost, Aura, the essence of life that defines you, can enter this universe of light; hence you call it heaven. However, this machine can transform the atoms in your body into a substance of light that can skim the face of the veil without completely penetrating it. Your consciousness can then direct you to any time or place you desire and return by way of the energy transmitted from the nearest portal available, and there are many portals. I'm sure you're very familiar with some of them as an archeologist. They are all recognizable to you as ancient, historical sites like Stonehenge, the pyramids of Egypt, South America, Asia, Antarctica." This statement startled Ruth.

"Antarctica!"

"Oh, of course, many of these passages have not been discovered in this time period, forgive me. First, place the artifact in its allotted place on the outer structure." He pointed to the area. "When the structure has accepted the artifact, touch these symbols on its face in this sequence." He pointed to the specific markings in sequence. Then place your hand on its center. It will act like a highly sophisticated bar code reader enabling it to analyze and transform your very being into a creation, unlike anything you could imagine. You will experience every atom in your body vibrating, don't worry, that is a normal reaction."

"I'm not stupid. What you failed to mention is vibration causes friction, and friction will cause heat, and heat can burn."

"This is true, but the atoms in your body, through the aid of the machine, will vibrate at precisely the correct frequency required to blend into your new surroundings."

"I must give you an A for your explanation. You do tell a convincing story, but I know it's full of crap, and so do you. So, I'm waiting for the punch line." Peter beckoned her to continue. Filled with skepticism, she was intrigued to hear his next explanation. Touching the symbols he'd shown her, she then placed her hand on the stone. Her thoughts were, 'how's he going to explain the next non-event?' A tingling sensation pulsed through her very being. Seeing her body start to emit light startled her. Within a split second, she had become an incandescent golden glow emanating bright incandescent sparks. This was definitely not what she'd anticipated. Once a dull rock face, the portal inside the door frame had become an opalescent wall resembling mother-of-pearl. Its subtle luminescence contained the full collar spectrum. It then transformed into a view screen of the place and time her thoughts had imagined. She stepped through.

"Remember what you see is now only in the Now or the present, you may wish to call it. So choose your thoughts wisely, the past is but a memory, the future a dream, and we all know how memory can play tricks with our thought process. I did not tell you this before, and I know you will eventually ask; your body has been destroyed, but don't be alarmed."

"You've just got me killed, and you say I'm not to be alarmed." Her anger and frustrations were starting to erupt.

"Do not be concerned. When we re-enter the new Now, our bodies will reconstruct to the exact specifications initially entered into its memory, aided by the machine. It will be created from identical materials readily at hand throughout the universe. You will be immediately reincarnated."

She felt an overwhelming need to put this theory to the test. Although there was a sense of warmth and security in this passageway of light.

CHAPTER 2

⛩

Seeing the Acropolis's steps before her, with a sensation much like stepping off an escalator, she walked towards them. Simultaneously she checked her physical form. Everything seemed to be in place. Looking around, the now-familiar figure of her companion, Gates, was close at hand. He, however, was dressed in white robes, as was she. Viewing herself with arms slightly raised, she looked to him with an expression that begged an explanation.

"Yes, the machine compensates. It would be unwise and dangerous to show up looking out of place and out of time with one's surroundings. Wouldn't you agree? It sometimes also supplies currency and tools when deemed necessary."

"This is fantastic ancient Greece, The Acropolis." She spun around with arms outstretched, in awe of her surroundings. Together they slowly walked around the main building. Its polished white stone glistened in the sunlight. The Marble's stark whiteness was dazzling to the eye, so much in contrast to the deep blue late afternoon sky. She absorbed every detail; only her imagination had allowed until now. These monuments displayed before her were real to view and touch. Ruth felt compelled to reach out and fill their texture. They moved on.

"

"We've reached the far side. This section of the mount is an old fortification, perhaps the first of many man-made structures. With this view, it's easy to see the strategic value of such a vantage point."

Peter then decided this pause in their walk was over. They continued until they arrived at the front of the main building once more.

"We seemed to have attracted the attention of that group of people over there. How should we react if they speak to us?"

"You won't find that a problem. The machine compensates for the language difference. You'll find yourself fluent in the tongue spoken in the time and place that has become your Now."

"If the machine consists of a group of ancient artifacts, how can it still function when they are in such decay? Why has it not been maintained?"

"Questions, questions. The machine is in immaculate condition in its Now, but not your Now of origin. In your, Now, it conforms to its surroundings. It would create too much attention not to have aged in your Now. Please rethink your concept of time. It's merely an illusion."

"A young man from that group is approaching us. This will be interesting. I'm sure any conversation we might have will be vastly different from anything I've experienced before."

"Greetings, my name is Pericles, son of Xanthiops. I believe you are strangers to these parts. I would not have forgotten such a daughter of Athena as yourself. Also, your companion's looks are quite distinctive. Do you travel from afar, and if so, is this your first visit to our beautiful city?"

Peter whispered in her ear. "I think he just asked if you come here often. Well, that's a pickup line I bet you've never heard before." Ruth nudged her elbow into his ribs.

"Greetings, my name is Ruth, and this is my companion, Peter."

"Peter, are you from Israel or thereabouts?"

"No. I am from a land far to the west. It is beyond the Mediterranean Sea and across a great Ocean that lays beyond." Pericles looked puzzled.

"This land you speak of is not known to me." There was an air of doubt in his tone that questioned the validity of this statement. He quickly changed the subject. "Then are you here for this evening theatrical performance."

"Yes, we're here to experience tonight's performance."

"Perhaps then you will allow me the privilege of extending you an invitation to join me as my friends."

"That would be very gracious of you," Ruth replied, knowing it was she that held his interest.

Ignoring Peter in an almost condescending manner, Pericles held out his hand for Ruth to place hers upon, which she graciously accepted.

"Let us move on to the amphitheatre, we will be early, but that will give ample time to sit and enjoy a pleasant conversation. Please allow me a moment." He left her for an instant to summon his entourage. This allowed Ruth the opportunity to whisper to Peter.

"Why do you think he questioned your name, Peter?"

"I don't know, but please understand Peter's more of a title than a name, you know. Perhaps he wishes me to feel uneasy and views me as a rival for your affections."

The entourage had arrived to start the walk down to the amphitheatre. Pericles again offered his hand to Ruth. As they walked, Pericles spoke of his dreams and aspirations.

"I've decided I will not take the crown of Athens. I believe that governance should be shared. Yes, it will be administered by a Senate made up of open-minded men. Scientists, philosophers, artists all will have their place in this new government. This will be a time of enlightenment, a beacon for democracy. The start of a new era for civilization."

"Those thoughts are admirable. I'm sure Athens will be regarded as the birthplace of this new democracy you speak of, and you, one of its creators."

Ruth's inner thoughts were Pericles was a very astute diplomat. He would undoubtedly distribute any bad decisions amongst the government and quite probably take credit for any popular ones himself. This form of governance would also help insulate him from outside criticism. However, they were the guests of this powerful politician, and any type of understanding of politics by a woman would probably not be looked upon as acceptable in this era.'

Pericles continued taking. "That would be a fitting legacy for any mortal. I could not wish for more."

As they took their seats, a small group of men positioned themselves close behind and near the stairway. Peter alerted Ruth to what he considered a potential situation. "I believe there are Spartans in our misted."

"Spartans, are you sure?"

"I spent enough time with three hundred of them in another place and time to appreciate their discipline and mannerisms." Ruth quickly picked up on an arising situation that would see Pericles and his party effectively screened and isolated by this small band of men in this crowded amphitheatre. As one moved into a position close to Pericles, she used her body as a human shield as she shouted to the crowd around them.

"Assassins, Spartan assassins." This distraction allowed Peter to physically restrain this would-be assassin long enough for others in the audience to react. By sheer weight of numbers, the Spartans were soon overwhelmed. These would-be assailants were then placed under arrest.

Their well-laid plan to attack Pericles had been completely defused by Ruth's heroism. This unselfish act had thwarted this would-be assassination attempt. Only in the aftermath of this heated exchange was Pericles able to realize the precarious position he'd been placed in.

"I am forever in your debt. All Athens is in your debt. Spartan politics can most often be more violent than alternative diplomatic solutions. Another excellent reason to pursue this new democracy I have planned. It would be harder to assassinate a whole Senate than just one man. How fortunate am I to have met such a brave and beautiful woman at such an opportune time."

Ruth's thoughts were somewhat different. (I think I've already figured out how this man's mind works and how he intends to govern. He can rule the roost from behind the crowd giving himself much more security. Yes, that's it; he's running true to form, a typical politician.)

Ruth's appreciation was extended to some grandiose gestures, which climaxed with a kiss on the hand. Peter, however, received a quick but appreciative thank you.

"I think I've lost the enthusiasm for entertainment in a crowded place this evening. Perhaps I can extend an invitation to yourself and Peter to join my friends and me at my villa."

"That's very kind of you. I would love the opportunity to join you, but as we came to see tonight's performance, perhaps another time."

"Then, Until we meet again." Pericles kissed her hand once more before he and his entourage departed.

Ruth was then thrilled to witness a Greek tragedy unfold before her eyes by actors who had finely honed this art form. When the show had finished and the night had closed in, they decided it was time to leave this place. Well, making their way back to the portal, their conversation turned to the interpretation of all recent events.

"Quite a successful day, I'd say. Your first excursion and you stopped an assassination that would have disrupted a Now that will alter humanity.

In this Now, it is a pivotal point at which a new strategy to govern a democratic society was created."

"You told me that only Now matters, and there is no past or future."

"Well, yes and no. It's complicated. Think of this Now as a leaf in a book. Without that page, the book becomes incomplete. You have much to learn, and it will take time, but time is something we have an abundance of. So think of another now you would like to visit."

"Perhaps we should take Pericles up no his offer. I'd like to see more of this now."

"Then stay; we will and enjoy this experience until you feel it's time to leave."

CHAPTER 3

After spending time as guests of Pericles, it was decided it was time to move on. Peter suggested she should think of a destination, and he would follow. Returning to the portal, Ruth entered then emerged from the doorway near the mountain's dig site they had recently left. Only seconds had passed in this time since she and Peter had departed for their adventure in Athens.

"Why did you return here, Ruth? We should have gone anywhere but here. There are so many other Nows to explore before you are ready to revisit this place. It is not a safe place for you at present. We should leave imediatly.

"But I'm happy here. This is the place I want to be. This work excites me. It's always been my life's ambition. Why wouldn't I want to be here? Yes, Athens was a unique experience that I will never forget, but this is where I belong. Exploring the past through astrology and piecing it together to understand how it has shaped mankind excites me much more than living it. I've never aspired to be a participant in every epic historical event I could imagine. And why do you say this is not a safe place for us to be. There's nothing here that poses a threat, surely?"

"Your welfare will always be a top priority to me, Ruth. Please, I implore you; let's leave. There's no time to explain. Just accept this as fact. This is not a good place for you to be right now. We should leave immediately. It wasn't some chance encounter that first brought me here. It's your destiny to explore time and space, so please let's go explore."

"What is so important that makes it imperative we leave right now."

"Your future depends on you leaving this place, Ruth. One day you will understand. There's so much for you to learn. Right now is not the time or place to continue your lessons. So please take the lead, and I'll follow."

She looked surprised by his persistence. "I thought you explained how irrelevant time was, and only, the Now is important. So why is it so important we leave this Now immediately?"

"Because this Now is a place you need to be when other Now's, have given you the experience to deal with this situation."

"That statement probably makes sense to you, but I have no idea what you're talking about. So until you give me some kind of explanation, I'm not going anywhere."

"There are events about to unfold which should not and must not be changed. You have already glimpsed how small interventions can change the entire course of history."

"This Now is becoming history by the second, but there is a future here for me. Why would it not be prudent for me to live that future? After all, as you say, only, Now is important."

"This may be your Now, but remember this; time has no boundaries. Your present time is someone else's past. Think of time as a book. By deleting a sentence or a paragraph, the story becomes incomplete. Your participation in this tale is an important one. It is a story that must be told in full. We will return here many times, but we will pick those times carefully."

"As you wish. It must be important for you to be so insistent, and as you say, we can return here at any time." She reached out her hand to Peter as she did once before, and together they walked towards the portal.

"Where is it to be this time, Ruth? There are billions upon billions of destinations waiting to be explored. Each Now is like a picture, photographs all set out on a table, every second of time recorded simultaneously, and all of them set to follow the course they are distend to follow."

As they walked towards the portal, she thought she heard the sound of thunder in the distance. Perhaps there's a storm on the horizon. That would be a good enough reason to leave, she thought to herself. Her imagination then centred on a destination that would intrigue her. Stone Heng, yes, I'd love to see Stone Heng in all its glory. She'd committed herself to enter the portal still hand in hand with Peter. Both of their free hands pierced the veil simultaneously. In that instance, as they were drawn through together, she perceived something strange. Several bright flashes followed by loud bangs. It was a noise that more resembled explosions than thunder and lightning. These disturbances were coming from the vicinity of the base camp further down the mountain. It was too late to go back as they were drawn in and transported to their destination. Although the lights and sounds she'd experienced puzzled her, it no longer felt relevant. After all, she could always return to that Now any time she pleased.

CHAPTER 4

Stone Heng surrounded them as they exited the portal. Their exit was accompanied in the same stepping off an escalator sensation Ruth had experienced when visiting Athens. She walked away from the site to view it in all its glory. She then walked back to be close enough to touch the stones. Although it was an ancient monument on their visit, it was still retained its pristine condition. This gave her a clearer perspective on the precision achieved by its builders. Being at Stone Heng itself was more like a spiritual experience for Ruth. It gave her a sense of tranquillity. It was a sensation no time-weathered photograph of the site could possibly achieve. Although never setting foot here before, she sensed an air of familiarity about the place. It was just one of those day-java moments, she thought and brushed it off as being no more than that. After a quick inspection of the monument, the urge to move on became overwhelming. However, she did know exactly which direction to take when choosing one of several paths leading away from the site.

"Let's make for the coast, Peter."

"Well, this was a fleeting visit to the Heng. As an archeologist, I wouldn't have thought you'd have been so quickly bored with this place?"

"I know I'll be here again, and there's this feeling of urgency we should be making for the coast."

"That's good you're starting to have such thoughts. It's all part of your learning process."

"You keep talking about this learning process, so please tell me more about it and what I'm supposed to be learning. Please enlighten me as we walk."

"There's little to tell, it's more of a self-education process, and I believe you're a fast learner."

"Sometimes you really piss me off the way you always answer my questions with riddles or innuendos. It makes me feel like you're constantly talking down to me."

"I'm sorry, I didn't mean to be rude or make fun. It's just sometimes intuition makes understanding the intangible easier to explain than words could ever do. It's starting to unfold before you, but you must be patient. Don't force it."

"Don't force what?"

"There you go again. Just let things happen. They will happen."

"Well." She turned her head and held her nose high in the air. "I can see this conversation's going nowhere." She had this feeling of disdain about her and a disgruntled attitude to match. Although the thought of several days of challenging trekking soon quailed Ruth's frustrations.

"Do you know yet why we need to go to the coast?"

"I'm getting this overwhelming sense of anxiety. Someone needs our help, and it is urgent."

A shroud of mist gathered as they neared the sea. "This way, Peter, we're nearly there." He smiled.

"Led on, Ruth." She walked towards a sheltered hollow in the dunes that overlooked the shore. A person was lying huddled there. They were completely covered with a cloak. It seemed to have been placed there in a loving manner by some caring person. There was a slight movement beneath this garment, so Ruth spoke. "Are you well?" Can we assist you in any way?"

The wizened face of an old man appeared as he drew back the cloak and turned towards her. "I fear I am beyond your help, my dear. Age has a way of betraying all our bodies eventually. But if you can see it in your heart to help the boy in any way, you would be doing me a great service."

She noticed he held a tall pointed hat with gold inlaid markings close to his chest. It had a small brim. These ornate inlaid symbols must have a definite meaning, Ruth thought. She reached out to touch the hat, but he pulled away. "No, this is not for you."

"Your hat, sir, it's an almanac, is it not? You are a man of much wisdom. A Seer of your people."

In a weak and quivering voice, he replied." You also have this power, am I correct?" Ruth was about to disclaim this observation when Peter intervened.

"Her powers are still in bud, but yes, sir, you are correct."

"Then it was providence that sent you this way. You must spend my last hours with me, my child. I have much to tell you, and you, in turn, have much to learn." Ruth sat beside him as he slowly explained the many secrets the hat contained."

The riggers of this process had drained the little strength remaining in his old frail body, and he slipped into his final deep sleep.

A grave was dug for his last resting place, and after the burial, Peter said some appropriate words. "If we had a name, we could etch it on a rock."

"There is a name that comes to mind. At the moment of his passing, it was as though I was in a portal to greet him. As his light entered through, I greeted him to the other side by saying, well-come, Merlin. It was so strange, but it was just a silly illusion. It seemed so real, a very moving experience. The event took minutes to unfold. Yet it all happened in the blink of an eye. Is this something to do with that learning process you keep talking about?"

"I love that inquisitive mind of yours. However, you do not need me to confirm what you're already becoming aware of." This time she just grinned at him. This comment would have upset her enormously a day or so ago, but not today.

"We must wait here for the boy Peter. He will confirm his name. Carving that name into rock will be a task only he can fully cherish because it will be done with love."

"Then, we must wait."

The wait was a short one. Ruth and Peter were soon joined at the burial site by a congregation of people who arrived from all directions. It became apparent the word of Merlin's ailing condition had spread, and the source of this information must have been the boy Merlin spoke of. This was confirmed as the last group of people arrived with a young man in the led. A solemn reverence hung over the gathering as they stood around the gravesite.

"I'm too late. I knew when he sent me, I should not go." The young man's emotions finally had unleashed an uncontrollable flow of tears. His grief was torn between guilt and sorrow."

"He slipped away in his sleep. It was a peaceful passing. I hope that will give some comfort to your loss.

"Were you with him?"

"Yes, I stayed with him to the end."

"Then I thank you for that."

"Is your name Arthur.?" The young man looked surprised at the question.

"No. I do not know this Arthur you speak of. Why would you think that was my name?"

"I'm sorry I was confused, so may I ask your name, young man?"

"I am Merlin, son of Merlin. I was also my father's apprentice." Ruth's thoughts re-aligned her mistake. Right place, wrong time, or perhaps not.

"My friend Peter and I promised your father we would assist you in your training wherever possible."

"This crowd, you see before you looked to him for guidance. I'm sure they will now look to me, but I have not the wisdom required for this task."

"Then, we must start with you performing the ceremony over his grave for them. You will then place a marker of your making upon it." He nodded in compliance. You must also wear this hat, for your training has been accelerated. I believe that is the sole purpose of Peter and myself being here is to help in that process."

A simple ceremony was performed, after which the crowd slowly dispersed. The young Merlin was then allowed a period of personal grieving time before his schooling began.

***

Ruth's first tutorial for Merlin was to decipher the coding contained in the hat. This was the same knowledge Merlin senior had trusted Ruth with. There was also a wealth of information she possessed on minerals and rocks. A chemistry lesson she felt every shaman should have mastery of. Perter assigned himself the task of schooling Ruth in his knowledge of botany. This information was then to be passed on to Merlin. Any competent Chaman should be capable of making medicines and potions.

Also, he should have an intimate knowledge of fauna and flora. This would be invaluable in this art. Peter collected specimens and sorted them into specific groups. These were then handed over to Ruth. This allowed her to complete the task of relating this information to young Merlin. Ruth and Merlin had formed an extremely close bond in these long hours spent together. Ruth could see; for a young boy on the verge of manhood, this friendship was much different for him than for her.

Also, at this time, they had returned to the Heng. Once there, another essential part of his schooling was fully understanding its functions concerning astrology and the seasons. This also gave Ruth the much-needed time she required to pursue her passion, archaeology. Peter also gave Ruth the task of searching out herbs, roots and fungi for Merlin to catalogue for later reference.

An emotional attachment had now developed between Ruth and Merlin. Was this mothering instinct towards this handsome young man or something more. This problem intensified as, over time, she saw a lot of her own traits in his persona. Her feelings were perhaps becoming too entwined, and she decided to speak with Peter.

"I think we are at a stage in Merlin's education where he does not require further guidance from us. Do you agree?"

"I'm glad you've come to that decision yourself. I also think it's time for us to leave, but first, we will summon young Merlin's father's followers for the young man's inauguration ceremony at the Heng. We must see this episode through."

Arraignments were made, and a date was set. With her passion for archaeology, Ruth was thrilled at the thought of actually witnessing this ritual. For her, it would be like having a dream come true. She would also have enough knowledge of this ceremony to write a book on this subject alone. This could be her thesis. However, would this be ethical, and how could she explain such knowledge. There would have to be much thought and research to shroud the true origins of the information she was about to obtain. Yes, way too unethical for her to contemplate.

The ceremony was everything she had hope for and more. As proceedings came to a close, the participants led the followers away from the site in an orderly procession. This was a good time for Peter and Ruth to bid farewell to this place. There was the last glance by Merlin in the very instant they entered the portal. For him, it was as if they disappeared before his very eyes. A tear trickled down his cheek in this emotional moment. Merlin's perception as a Seer gave him a limited understanding of the situation, but this parting nevertheless was a sad one.

CHAPTER 5

In their haste to leave, little thought had been given to a new destination. Was this some random selection? Because it seemed to be an unexpected surprise to Peter and Ruth as they entered this, Now. Ruth had been thinking of Vancouver, Canada. This was a place she had once visited on a cruise ship with her mother. However, this was not a Vancouver she recognized. The portal from which they had made their exit seemed to be in a museum. It was situated near a window. She moved closer to get a better view. The only thing familiar was the profile of the north shore mountains. The living space and workspace of the downtown core were integrated into a landscape of parks and forests. Much like the Hobbits village in Lord of the rings, a book she had read. At a quick glance from a distance, the building could easily be mistaken for foothills of mountain ranges to the north and east. Roadways were almost indistinguishable under the forest's canopy that bordered them as they disappeared and reappeared through city structures. The main arteries ran east to west at an elevated level. North to south running roads were situated on levels below.

Interchanges were facilitated by vehicles merely sidestepping their glide way, then dropping or rising to the appropriate level and direction.

Some glide ways terminated at the more significant buildings. The would-be cars were also much different from anything she'd ever seen before. There was no trunk or hood, and the most striking difference, there were no wheels. They hovered just above the road surface, gliding smoothly and silently to their destinations. When the occupants exited a vehicle, the roof telescoped into the seating area, and the whole thing upended itself to be stored together like large packs of playing cards. They did not seem to be individually owned but rather personalized community transportation to be used at will.

"Peter, what's happened? Where are we?"

"You've chosen what would be for you a future Now."

"How can that be? I have no knowledge of this place. How could I have imagined a place I have no idea had ever existed."

"As I've said before, forget every concept of time you've ever had. Each time is Now that's how we go from one place to another so smoothly. This place we're in seems to be a museum. I think we've visited the perfect site. Look around; it should be a great eye-opener for you. Learn what you can well we're here. I'm sure there's a host of things you'll find extremely informative in a place like this. I have something I wish to see, so shall we meet back here in two hours."

Ruth decided to steer clear of archaeology for the time being. She headed for the museum's engineering galleries. The mechanics of cars that move without wheels was Ruth's intention to explore first when entering this section. This section seemed to cover every aspect of engineering imaginable. "Ask me your question," she was told by an interactive hologram as she walked into its reception area. My interests are in the mechanics of modern vehicles. This hologram then presented and explained the subject matter requested by Ruth.

It described how supercooled circular magnetic conductors enabled the movement of heavy loads over lightly coated in Alumina-based material. Another exhibit explained how two discs, spinning counter-clockwise to each other at an incredible speed, could produce a magnetic field capable of diffing gravity. The discs themselves were kept floating apart by supper cooled nitrogen, and the mechanisms to spin them in opposing directions were linear motors. This structure was mounted inside a tubular-type housing.

These were more than just diagrams drawn up before her. They were full-scale models that could be blown apart to explain any part of the selected project's inner workings that she needed clarification on. The secrets of cold fusion had also been unravelled in this future Now. Conservation, sustainability, and self-sufficiency were a code this generation adhered to as its bible.

After leaving this gallery, Ruth visited another one that took her interest. This gallery was dedicated to art. She was pleased to see this form of creativity had not been neglected in this specific time. It still played an intricate and essential part in this society's social pleasures. It was a fascinating and enjoyable place for her to explore, and the hours passed quickly.

When eventually meeting up with Peter, food was the first thing on her mind. "Can we eat now, Peter? I'm so hungry."

"I'm hungry too, but the food in this cafeteria may not be exactly like the food you're accustomed to. However, I'm sure you'll find it very tasty and as hungry as we are, I'm sure it'll hit the spot."

Peter was correct as usual: The food was different and varied in so many ways. The presentation was exquisite. Ruth's mouth watered at these culinary works of art. Everything on the menu had been harvested from the gardens on top of the complex and its greenhouses within. Over lunch, Peter made a few suggestions to Ruth.

"Is your knowledge of minerals and geology as good as it should be?"

"That's a strange question, but yes, I try to keep abreast of things in that field, Peter. Why do you ask?"

"They have a wonderful gallery devoted to that subject, and I know your archeological knowledge must border on that, so I thought you might find it interesting. I'm heading towards the botany section to check it out. I don't think that holds much interest for you. Am I correct?"

"OK, I know when I'm being dumped. See you back here in an hour."

It was strange that Ruth became so engrossed in this subject so quickly. It was as if it was a subject she would need to use very soon. Had Peter steered her this way for a reason? If so, what did he know that she didn't? Oh well, she thought, if I asked, I suppose he'd only tell me to relax, and it'll all become clear to me eventually.

Peter showed up for a coffee sometime before Ruth.

"You're running a little late, Ruth." Peter tried to fain a stern look.

"How's that possible time's irrelevant, and I quote you on this matter; because those are your very words." They both laughed.

"You have me there, Ruth. Now, I will stay with you here for a few days. Then I have pressing business to attend to, so I will be leaving you here. Study for a while before you move on. There are hotels close by where we can stay. I'm sure we can book you into one at the reception of this facility. Learn all you can in this Now, before you leave. Then you should probably make your next excursion to another, Now alone. Just another part of your learning experience." He gave her a grin, "You know where the portal is. We'll meet up back here before our next trip together."

"O-o-o. K. If you say that's all there is to it."

"How long should I stay here, Peter? How will I know where to meet you?"

"Perhaps a week or two after I leave would be an appropriate length time, and you'll know when it's time for you to leave."

"How will I just know."

"Trust me, Ruth, you just will. The next part about meeting up is easy. Ruth, just think of me, or I will think of you, and we'll be here to meet each other. Oh, one more thing, do not go past the portal in the archeological section; it is imperative, am I clear." She did not understand why, but she nodded in compliance.

"There's also an advanced learning process available in the hotel. It will allow you to absorb information quickly. Take full advantage of it. There's a sleep system installed near your bed that helps accelerated learning. It responds to any subject of your choice. It will take place as you slumber. Unlike like dreams, which are random, it allows you to organize your learning process on the chosen subject."

"So, it's like a sound-induced indoctrination."

"Slightly more sophisticated than that. More like telepathy is the best way I can explain it to you. A single night's course would be the equivalent of a full semester of college in your now. So, I strongly suggest you make full use of this opportunity."

Several days later, Peter explained to Ruth it was time for him to leave. She turned away just for a moment, and he had unceremoniously vanished. He'd slipped away, back to the portal to visit another Now perhaps. Or was this other business he had to attend to maybe something entirely different. This all seemed a little strange and unusual. It also felt a little unnerving, alone in this strange place and time: But she took Peter's advice to glean as much information from this Now as possible before the urge to leave consumed her.

CHAPTER 6

Entering the museum's portal, Ruth exited through another gate carved into one side of a large crevice in a cliff face. It seemed to Ruth to be familiar as she perceived it to be identical to the one in the museum. This exit was again a similar experience that Ruth was becoming accustomed to. In the same manner, Peter had apparently left the museum some days before Ruth in the same way. However, She did not know his new destination. This somehow didn't seem to bother her one bit. She was confident that he would be there for her when she needed to see him again. Making her way to the cliff face, she peered out to check her new location. This was a strange and rugged place she'd arrived at. Below her, the base of a massive gorge opened up into a valley. The other direction seemed to ascend to perhaps the moors above. Vegetation was sparse. The gate's remote location would seem to have been built with the specific intention of being totally obscured from any unwelcome viewing from the gorge floor below.

Neither a time nor place had entered her thoughts this time. It was just the image of one person that had occupied her mind; young Merlin. How could this be, just another thing for Perter to explain at their next meeting? Yes, right, she then thought, as she had a chuckle to herself about the obvious reply to her question would be.

The vision of this young man had somehow consumed her thoughts after Peter had left her so abruptly. Feeling assured that they would meet up at the museum after this excursion, it seemed a good time for some personal time. Separation for a while could prove to be a good thing. Even the closest of friends need time apart to maintain their real individuality and perspectives on life. Ruth now considered Peter to be in the category of a confidant and friend she could trust with her life.

Walking out from the craves, she surveyed her new surroundings. Although bleak and rugged, this area had an air of tranquillity about it. She'd then found herself on a path that approached the mouth of a rocky gorge. Once on the valley floor, Instinctively, she knew her way, lay forward and up this steep ravine.

Water from a spring spurting from the rock face fed a Chrystal clear brook that bubbled and churned its way down through the gorge. Several large caves penetrated deep into the rock face near this water sores. The larger cave of two nearby commanded her attention.

Intuition dictated this was the place she was destined to visit. As she entered its mouth, a familiar face emerged from its darkness to greet her.

"Ruth, this cannot be. It was twenty years and more since you tutored me. Yet here you are, still, that beautiful young woman I remembered you to be. Again how can this be? It is beyond belief." She felt this strange bond of affection between them rapidly developing into something more than just the friendship that was.

"Just accept it as fact, Merlin. Now look at you; no longer that gangly young lad I first meet. You've developed into this handsome, fully mature manly figure I see before me today." She took his hands in hers as they pulled apart for a full view of each other. This statement was made with much emotion. Merlin sensed more in Ruth's warmth towards him than one of just an old friend. "Time's favoured you well, Merlin."

"As it has you, Ruth. Your Beauty still bedazzles me. In my memory, I suppose it always has. Seeing you again has reawakened those thoughts. When you left on that day so long ago, you stole a piece of this broken heart of mine. You've held it captive ever since. Once broken, this same heart now rejoices in the knowledge that the secret pledge I made to myself so many years ago can now bear fruit. Ruth, you were my first and only love. I've always dreamed this day would come, and here you are standing before me. I also know you must have a purpose here, but I will take advantage of this time together, which is also our time. I'm sure you sense that too."

"Yes, I do, Merlin."

This feeling of incredible love increased as she placed her hands on his shoulders and gently kissed him on his cheek. As she did so, she felt his arms encompass her. His kiss was a much more passionate one. She did not resist because it no longer felt wrong. The time was now, and this Now was their Now, which made it right for both of them. Taking her by the hand, he led her into the cave. "Come, Ruth, this is my home. I knew this day would come as a seer, but reality told me it was impossible, yet here we are. I want you so much, Ruth. I've always loved you; I always will. As a boy, this could not be. Now I am a man, so all this is right, is it not? Come to my bed and let our passions engulf us as we quench the thirst of love that pulses from our inner souls. She affectionately snuggled close as they walked to his bed, intensifying this growing bond that, for him, had endured the test of time. Their resting place for love was built from ruff timbers with a mattress of stroll and fur and supported beneath with intertwining ropes. Disrobing, Merlin then seized the opportunity to assist Ruth. His hands explored every curve of her body as her garments fell to the floor one by one. Simultaneously the back of her neck was ingratiated by his lips. He then gently laid her beneath him on his soft matrice of fur. His fingers continued exploring Ruth's more intimate inner body as she seethed in raptures under his passion. His lips and tongue caressed her breasts before moving on to her lips as he slowly gently entered her body. She rose beneath him then fell away, encouraging him to follow, which he did. From the hearth, centred near the cave's entrance, firelight flickered on their bodies, glistening with sweat. The flame's erratic flickers and crackling almost seemed in tune with their inconstant dance of love. She felt a more comforting heat from him deep inside her than the warmth from this fire could ever give. As their passion subsided, so did their strength and sleep took hold.

Morning's first light pierced the cave entrance sparking Merlin to embark on the same passionate voyage so much enjoyed that previous evening. Ruth was more than willing to accommodate his needs, for they were also her needs. Once more, they resumed their intricate dance of love. The choreography of this rhapsody was enhanced by the understanding of each other's needs. It enriched the deeper bond only true lovers can possibly appreciate.

Ruth knew this love affair must be a fleeting one. She was here for a purpose and was sure that purpose would soon be reviled. Until such times she intended living this Now, this life, to the fullest. Seize the moment was foremost in her thoughts. Merlin was hers to love and appreciate. He commanded her love and controlled the very essence that was Ruth, in this Now. Merlin catered to her every need in return for this devotion lavished upon him. However, Ruth's demands sapped even his strength and stamina. Yet even this state of exhaustion could not stop their mutual needs. The compromise was a slower, gentler, more caring lovemaking than they'd previously enjoyed. This very slow, more sedate intimacy was accompanied by excessive caressing with lips and hands, contrasting with their previous needs. It gave a completely different perspective on their love for each other.

This moment produced memories within Ruth she did not realize excised. Memories of times past, present and future seemed to roll into one. This scenario had all been played out before. It was an experience she would return to time and again from a future or past Now. Peter had told her: Time and space are only illusions, and it all started to make some kind of strange sense to her. This would no longer be a fleeting romance but a cherished moment she could rekindle time and again. As time progressed, these day-Javier moments became more vivid and frequent, with recollections so sharp as to make these thoughts real memories.

Peter had told her this is how things would fall into place for her. Relaxation seemed to be the key to this process. Just let things happen, he said, and she was never more relaxed than in this now when she was in Merlin's arms. This was right; this was how things were meant to be. Merlin, her one and only true love, would be forever in her heart, as she would be in his.

Armed with this knowledge, Ruth also knew this love affair of ships passing in the night could be replayed, time over time. This knowledge gave her great comfort.

* * * * * * * * *

Merlin made himself busy preparing a breakfast of grains and herbs. Ruth decided to bathe in the crystal clear waters of one of the cave's many basins. Basins of this nature had formed by the constant drip drip drip from stalactites depositing their mineral-rich liquids to the cave floor. So many Stalagmites and Stalactites had developed by this same process.

"Choose the small basin Ruth and use hot rocks from the hearth to warm the water. It will make your bath time much more enjoyable, I assure you."

"Thanks, Merlin; I would have never have thought of that. What a great ideal."

"Use the large tongs near the hearth to move the rocks. If you find the task too hard, I will assist you."

"It's fine. I think I can manage."

After her bath, Ruth steeped from the basin. These white marble-like structures around her acted as mirrors reflecting the flickering flames of Merlin's fire. This same light reflected favourably on her exquisite form. A view that did not go unnoticed by Merlin. She then moved to where Merlin had laid out a bench made from rocks and covered by fur for them to sit.

Sitting close together in an affectionate snuggle, they shared the breakfast of tasty gruel from one wooden ball with two spoons. Merlin had hand-carved these wooded utensils exquisitely. Being an accomplished artisan in the art of working wood was just another aspect of the many talents he could turn his hands to. Ruth was fully aware of another use for this craftsman's hands as an affectionate smile came to her face.

Breakfast finished, Ruth took full advantage of this short time together by enticing Merlin back to bed to continue this marathon of passion. This time they experimented in every aspect of lovemaking conceivable to the imagination. It was an incredibly fulfilling time for both of them, time well spent investigating this tango of innovation.

CHAPTER 7

It was near noon before they emerged from the cave entrance. Steam rose from the gorge as the sun's rays worked the magic of nature upon the moisture deposited by a light morning shower. The smell of moist vegetation gave the fragrance of rebirth to this rugged wild place called the Cheddar gorge.

"Come, Ruth, I've something I wish to show you. It's a rock but not just any rock. This rock bears an ancient legend. It's said that he who can draw the sword from this stone will unite this land of Britannia and rule it as its greatest King." Ruth was starting to get an inclination of why she was here in this spot, and at this time.

Merlin guided her upwards through the gorge to the exact location where he said they would find the rock. There it was, this dark red collared rock in the misted of these white chalk hills, truly an anomaly in its own right. Ruth scrutinized the boulder, her knowledge in archaeology gave her great insight into geology. Inlaid into one face of this balder was a vivid shiny light grey effigy resembling a sword.

"There's the sword Ruth. Do you see the dilemma? It would be an impossible task to try removing it."

"This rock is haematite, iron ore of the finest quality, and the sword, I believe, is a chromium deposit. I know how to extract the sword from this stone, Merlin. It will take your skills as an engineer, plus my knowledge of the smelting process and hard work. Also, other elements must be acquired to extract the sword from this stone correctly. Bauxite and bentonite clays, Limestone, Sand, and that black rock that burns so well in your hearth is anthracite coal. I need as much of that as you can acquire. The hard work we'll leave to the young Arthur. This is his birthright."

"Who is this Arthur you speak of? I remember you called me by that name the very first time we met. You mistook me for him, as I recall. There must be some great significance regarding this person's destiny."

"Yes, he's the son of Uthur Pendragon. I believe perhaps it was your father who was an adviser to that King. When your father passed away, I thought it would fall to Peter and myself to tutor Arthur, but I was mistaken. We were there as your tutors. It will be your destiny to mentor this young prince and help mould him into the man he is destined to become. He will be that great King you spoke of, and you'll be the power behind that thrown. The purpose of Peter and myself all those years ago was to tutor you in preparation for this time. You will be the mentor to that great King. His faith, Christianity, will also be a deciding factor in his rain as King. You'll teach him a different method of governance. It will be done by consensus at a round table by knights of the land. It will also be his destiny to establish a code of honour. It will be called Chivalry. My purpose here today is to help produce a great sword for him. This sword will be the symbol of the King's great power. It's all becoming quite clear to me now. We must return to the cave and draw up plans for the furnace. You will then build it, and I will seek out the materials we will need for the smelting process."

"You speak of strange things, Ruth. Where did you acquire all this knowledge? You also have great insight into the future. Is it sorcery?"

"Do I look or act like a witch? because I assure you that is not the source of my knowledge."

"Well, you have beguiled me, you beautiful woman."

"Guilty as charged on that count, I hope." she snuggled close and gave him a hug, which was reciprocated.

They came upon a young man waiting outside as they approached the cave.

"I was told by the monks at Old Saram to seek out Merlin, the magician, and that I would find him in this place. Are you he?"

I am Merlin, seer of my people. A man at one with nature, but no magician, although I believe it is I you seek. I am aware of your purpose.

This fine lady is Ruth. She is also here to aid you, Prince Arthur. For that is who you are, is it not?"

"If you are not a magician, how did you know my name and my purpose ?" Ruth grind.

"I think he's got you there, Merlin. This should be fun seeing you talk your way out of this one."

"This one; what is the meaning of this one, Lady Ruth? You speak in a strange tongue with strange words."

"Yes, perhaps I do, but there's much for you to learn, Arthur, and we will be your tutors."

"But I have finished my tutoring. That is why the monks sent me here after my uncle died. As the son of Uthur Pendragon, I wish to establish my birthright, and I was told you would assist me in my quest."

"We will, but your quest will start with you accompanying me in my quest, which is to seek out materials for an important project. A project that will help fulfil a prophecy on its completion. It will inequitably establish your right to the throne. Consider this trip part of your tuition, as I will teach you many things along the way. Merlin will work his magic on building something we'll need in the first steps to fulfil your destiny. You and I will be responsible for acquiring the ingredients necessary to facilitate this process. A process that will truly amaze you, but there is more than enough time well on our quest for me to school you in that process also."

"Then he is a magician. You said he is about to work magic." This time it was Merlin's turn to laugh.

"I'm looking forward to hearing your explanation about this statement, my Lady Ruth."

"Well, Merlin, could you explain the magic you've worked on me since I've been here. As for my own explanation, I'll leave that too much later, boys. Right now, there's work to be done."

Inside the cave, Ruth found parchment, a pen, and ink. Merlin was also something of a scribe and had frequent uses for such things. She began preparing drawings for a furnace, waterwheel, and bellows. The bellows were a challenge as Ruth needed continuous airflow to the cupola to produce such high heat. She came up with a two bellow system that comprised of a double bellow construction in each pair. The middle board would also be incorporated into a stabilizing table. An arm connected to a cam on the extended shaft of the water wheel pumped down the upper side, and as one double would open, the counter side of the same double beneath it utilizing a connecting arm would collect air in the lower section. Thus continuing this process on the lower bellow as the wheel continued its turning momentum. This moved the arm up and down in a piston-like motion. It would give that much-needed continuous flow of air. The matching set of bellows would be mounted to the opposite side of the shaft utilizing another cam to perform the same operation. The compressed air would then be delivered by pipes made of brick and clay to the furnace. The furnace would be double-walled, having its cavity filled with sand mixed with bentonite clay for insulation. Its base would be made of bentonite clay, an excellent refractory material. To Ruth, this all seemed to be a very efficient design.

Merlin and Arthur had by now selected a site for this engineering feat and had cleared and levelled it. As daylight dwindled and evening shadows crept across the gorge, they retired to the cave for a meal, and what a meal it was.

Tending maturing cheeses stored in nearby caves was one of Merlin's many contributions to the community. This gave him access to a tasty food source. The most excellent cheese Cheddar could produce was laid out before them. Freshly baked bread was also on hand, all to be washed down by the exquisite elixir called cider. The production of this outstanding local drink was another task Merlin had a hand in. He'd also schooled the local population in the art of preserved jams made from local strawberries. Spread up on fresh bread, it would make an excellent dessert to round out their meal.

This was an excellent time to make plans for the following day, well enjoying this feast fit for a king. First, it was decided they would visit the local village to enlist help for this project. Hopefully, they could borrow a horse and cart to transport the materials needed for the project. Timber would be required for every aspect of this undertaking, from the wheel, the bellows and aqueduct construction for water delivery to the wheel. All this was labour intensive, and some strong arms would be needed to aid the work along. There were trees at the top of the gorge that could be cut for building timber. The black rock was brought from the north by traders. They also delivered clay for making pottery Merlin had told Ruth. This bentonite clay would also be needed in the making of the furnace. These traders would then barter it for cheese, dried fish, and preserves.

After supper, Merlin took stock of his tool collection. Ruth and Arthur cleaned supper utensils before making a bed for Arthur. As they worked, they talked. "Where would you prefer to sleep, young Prince Arthur." He pointed to an area close to where Merlin's bed was situated.

"That would seem to be as good a place as any." However, she had a nefarious interest in keeping as much distance as possible from where Merlin's bed was situated to where Arthur would be bedding down for the night. It was her intention to keep him as far away from them as possible. This would allow the privacy required for some uninterrupted boisterous lovemaking that she was hoping would occur.

"Merlin snores, you know. I don't think you would have a good night's rest so close. May I suggest that small alcove down that passageway? It should be well out of earshot."

"Earshot. What does that mean?"

"Far enough away to be undisturbed by any noise from our bed." He may have been young, but he was not naive. His slight blush soon turned to a smile.

"The alcove is a splendid idea."

The night went as planned for Ruth. It was everything she'd hoped for and more. Merlin had quickly mastered the techniques of innovation in the art of lovemaking. He was now something of an expert in pleasuring his true love in so many different ways. In catering to and fulfilling her every need, the gratification returned to him was the most significant high he could ever have imagined. As they reeled in ecstasy, hearts that once beat as one stumbled and fluttered into infrequency as oxygen-starved muscles struggled to maintain this state of euphoria, creating an even higher high as this deficiency also hit their brains. Reeling in this euphoric climax, complete and utter fulfilment rained. This satisfaction was accompanied by contentment and utter exhaustion. They fell to sleep in each other's embrace.

CHAPTER 8

The morning brought fresh challenges plus an informative visit to the nearby village of Cheddar. Ruth and Arthur were introduced to the locals, who immediately welcomed them into their community because of Merlin's close friendship. Also, the thought of a prince residing in their misted would give some notoriety to this somewhat sleepy village.

This tight community thrived on close co-operation, so any requests for help were quickly granted. The use of a donkey and cart was freely given, plus a young girl who owned the donkey volunteered her services as a guide. She then politely introduced herself.

"My name is Guinevere. I have a close bond with my donkey and do not like anyone else tending to Carrot. So I will join you on your quest." However, there was also an underlying motive for this offer. She'd taken a shine to young Arthur, and this trip would give her the perfect opportunity to forge a close friendship. This chance of some time away from mundane village life also appealed to her sense of adventure.

"Carrot, what a good name for a donkey Guinevere. Then I must give him one because I think he was named that for a good reason. He looks to be a grand pony who will serve us well, so I too would also like him as a friend." Arthur had a twinkle in his eye for this fair young lass, and flattery will get you everywhere sometimes. Arthur hopped perhaps this would be one of those times.

Preparations were then made for their quest, and all provisions assembled, plus camping needs, were packed onto the cart. The last thing Guinevere slid into one side of their mode of transportation was a stout staff.

"Why the staff?"

"It's for our protection Arthur. These hills are not always as friendly as they look to be. I'm well-schooled in its use. My great great great grandfather was a centurion in the Roman legions, and his fighting skills were legendary. Those skills have been passed down from father to son. Having no brothers, my father passed those skills on to me. Not being allowed the use of my father's sword, I make good use of my staff. A fighting staff is a great weapon in skilled hands." Arthur had some skepticism about this statement's bravado delivery. However, he smiled and nodded politely as not to offend. However, as striking a beautiful young woman Guinevere was, she was not a slightly built lass by any means. She was almost as large and imposing in stature as Arthur himself. Arthur also possessed other attributes, a poise that seemed to command respect was just one of them. This was a quality one would expect to find in a young, would be Monarch. This tall, handsome, strong, well proportioned young man also had many other attributes required for a future King's makings. These traits of regale deportment were also apparent in Guinevere.

As Merlin made preparations for his allotted assignment. Ruth's party made tracks west, searching for the materials required to facilitate the project's end goal. Ruth was confident limestone could be taken from the gorge itself, so that was not a priority. White sand, which mostly consisted of Quarts, would be easily acquired from one of the many beaches on the coast. So the mineral that would be hardest to locate in abundance would be bauxite.

As they walked, Ruth spoke of many things about the production of the sword. She was determined that Arthur would be quite capable of fulfilling all his required functions for its final manufacture. At that point, a medallion hanging on a leather thong around young Arthur's neck caught her attention. "The medallion around your neck; is it important to you."

"No, other than the fact it is silver and was given as a good luck charm. It holds no real meaning for me other than a memento of the person that gave it to me."

"Then may I look at it more closely." He took it off and passed it to her for a closer examination. "This could be very helpful in making the sword. I believe it's made of Nickle, another ingredient I was hoping to add to the steel alloy but didn't know where I would be able to acquire it."

"Then it is not silver."

"I don't believe so. It's a precious metal nonetheless but not silver."

"If it is important for our needs, then it is yours to do with as you will." She slipped it around her neck for safekeeping.

That evening they selected a campsite in a clearing close to a lake. Ruth intended to begin her search for some bauxite near this location the following day. Guinevere suggested she start a campfire, and Ruth could set up a shelter. Arthur was given the task of fetching water from the lake.

Only minutes had passed when Arthur's cries for help were heard coming from the lake. Rushing to his aid, both women saw Arthur floundering in the water.

"Help, I can not swim."

"Neither can I," replied Guinevere as Ruth quickly disrobed and dove in. After dragging young Arthur from the water, she looked at both of them in dismay.

"Right, the pair of you, Swimming lessons first thing tomorrow, no ifs and or buts about it."

"You speak with strange words again, Lady Ruth; what do they mean?"

"I will teach you to swim at first light."

"But the lake will be cold."

"That's where the ifs and buts come in; in short, no excuses."

The following morning Ruth had difficulty coaxing her unwilling pupils into the water. However, once in, they proved to be willing and enthusiastic students. They soon mastered the basics of swimming, and once that was achieved, Ruth then had trouble getting them out of the water. They wanted to stay and play, so Ruth gave up and left them to enjoy. She was confident either fatigue, or the cold would put an end to this leisure time.

"Lady Ruth, you saved my life and taught me to swim. Henceforth, I will refer to you as The Lady of the Lake, Lady Ruth. He took hold of Guinevere's staff and touched it on each of Ruth's shoulders. "I dub thee, Lady of the Lake. A well-earned title." She gave a little smirk to herself.

As Ruth searched for her bauxite, the two youngsters selected a sturdy sapling to make a stout staff for Arthur. Guinevere was determined to tutor Arthur in the use of the fighting staff. They spent the rest of the day engaged in mock combat. Guinevere proved to be every bit as good as she had claimed to be with the staff, and Arthur was acquiring bruises to prove it.

In the next few days, Ruth continued her search. The two youngsters continued their war games with intermittent dips in the lake to cool off. This was the time when Arthur and Guinevere cemented that close bond that would endure for the rest of their lives.

Eventually, Ruth found her precious bauxite. Everyone was tasked with making it into bricks and then setting it out to dry in the summer sun. As the blocks dried, the white effervescent substance formed on their exteriors. This substance was carefully scraped off and collected. This Ruth explained; would be added to the molten alloy in the furnace, hoping it would cause a chemical reaction that would raise the furnace temperature. A considerable amount of this substance, Ruth called alumina, would be required. She explained this knowledge to Arthur as alchemy, and she'd been taught it as part of her education.

When a cartload of bricks had been made, Guinevere was given the task of delivering them to Merlin to construct a furnace. Ruth and Arthur continued the task of collecting alumina, a time-consuming process. After taking a relaxing swim one evening, Arthur discovered a sandy beach on the lake. This sand would indeed save them a trip to the coast. Eager to tell Ruth, he arrived at the campsite at an opportune moment. Hearing Ruth's calls for help with staff in hand, he rushed to her aid. She was about to be set upon by a band of roaming brigands. "Throw bricks, Lady Ruth, defend yourself, have no fear I will handle these louts."

With his staff swinging to a rhythm taught in play, he converted that knowledge to practical use. With his newfound skills, he soon found targets such as knees, elbows and other vulnerable body parts to be speared. Ruth hurled bricks in a defence that proved to be a great distraction to their would-be assailants. Arthur was amazed at the staff's effectiveness in a skilled pair of hands proved to be. He quickly vanquished the last of the would-be villains. How valid Guinevere's words had proved to be and how glad was Arthur she'd taken the time to teach him those skills. He looked at Ruth with a sense of satisfaction in his smile. Only then did he ponder; what was this strange gesture she was making towards the fleeing rabble. She noticed his inquisitive look. "Oh, before you ask, it's called the one-finger salute. It means, well, um, forget what it means. It wasn't meant to be complimentary." He decided to let that subject drop.

"I think we will not see another visit from the likes of those villains again."

"I think you showed them who's the boss." He was about to ask for an explanation but then just shook his head and smiled knowingly instead.

Many more trips were made back to Cheddar before Ruth decided they had a sufficient amount of all the materials required, excluding the limestone. It was time to break camp. Their spirits were high as they made their way back to Cheddar.

CHAPTER 9

Ruth's return was expected, but nonetheless, still a pleasant respite in Merlin's day. Rushing into his arms the moment she saw him, he lifted her off her feet and spun her around in a show of joy and affection. "I know it's only been a short time, but I've missed you so much, Merlin. It feels so wonderful to be back here and have you hold me in this way. This is what I've really missed."

"I've mist you to Ruth, but we're so close to completion; let's save our real greetings until tonight when I can truly show you how much I've missed you." She pulled away and kissed him lightly on the cheek, but this was not his idea of a first greeting. A peck on the cheek was not about to satisfy his immediate needs. He pulled her back into a close embrace. This was followed by a shower of kisses and an outpouring of affection befitting the occasion. Merlin did this for her to sample his intentions for later that evening.

"I hope that's your way of letting me know that's just a taste of things to come? If so, I can't wait for tonight. You always have such a wonderful way of showing how much you care." Her statement was accompanied by subsidence in the outpouring emotions. She then fain-ed a limp faint in his arms. Ruth followed this with a smile that turned to laughter. When things had settled down to some kind of normality, Merlin explained that his projects were nearing completion. Within the hour, a trial run had been planned.

Ruth decided to use this time to make plans for Arthur's pending big day, but he and Guinevere were nowhere to be found. They'd slipped into one of the caves for some private time away from prying eyes.

* * * * *

"When I am King, I will need a Queen. Will you be that Queen, Guinevere?"

"You seem very confident about your destiny, my liege." This statement was made in jest-full banter.

"Would you have a man who was not prepared to seize that which was his by right of birth?" He placed a hand on her shoulder and placed a kiss upon her lips.

"So, am I also a birthright you are prepared to take." She said, continuing the banter before kissing him back. She then laughed and ran from the cave only to be waylaid by Ruth.

"So, having fun, were we?" A sheepish-looking Arthur then emerged. He got a look of scorn from Ruth.

"And you young man have better things to do with your time right now than canoodling. There will be time enough for that later, much later."

"Canoodling! what is the meaning of this word Lady Ruth?" She just laughed and beckoned him to move back to the worksite. "Go, young man. If you have that much energy, I have some hard work for you to do. Guinevere just laughed. "You too, young lady. Your not home free either."

"We do not understand your words, Lady Ruth."

"I'm sure you get my meaning if you get my drift." It was said in jest to amuse them. It did, and they both ran back to the worksite, swatting at each other. Ruth caught up with them there.

"Arthur, we have enough time before dusk for me to show you something. Then I'll explain your next project to you."

"I am eager to learn of this next undertaking I must complete, my Lady of the Lake." She took Arthur to the rock that bore the sword effigy. Word had obviously spread of the upcoming event. This had also become apparent by the influx of people at the mouth of the gorge. Several artists at the site sketched and painted pictures of the stone with the sword effigy in it. As a sign of politeness, Ruth and Arthur made a point of viewing each artist's works and comparing each one's merits. After these protocols had been observed, they again proceeded with the matters at hand. Ruth did her best to ignore the attention given to them, as she explained to Arthur his next assignment.

"Your task Arthur is a simple one. You must chisel all of the stone away from around the outside of the sword effigy. Save all the fragments; those chippings and more will be needed in your next undertaking. When that task's complete, the sword effigy must then be removed in one peace. We will then transfer everything to the furnace for smelting."

"This is an easy task you've set for me, but It will take time. I must also look my best as I am performing the work. These artists may wish to capture my efforts for everyone to view." Ruth rolled her eyes.

"Good grief, I have a primadonna on my hands, but you're right. It will take time and time we have in abundance, believe you me."

"Why should I not believe you, Lady Ruth."

"It's just a figure of speech, Arthur. It's just a meaningless comment."

"Then why do you say these meaningless words." She hugged him around the shoulder and gave him a smile. This gesture could not be misconstrued.

It was dusk when they arrived back at the base of the gorge. Merlin and the men of the village had taken a mountain goat with bow and arrow. It was to make a magnificent celebratory supper. They'd begun roasting it on a spit over an open fire. Vegetables were being prepared for boiling as a side dish. This smell of food was a welcome fragrance to hungry workers. A table and benches were quickly assembled from spare lumber, then set for the feast.

"Come, everyone, there is much to celebrate. Guinevere, Ruth, fetch cider." Ruth gave a scornful look.

"We are not wenches or servants of men. So ask politely, and we will do our part to help."

"It has been a long hard day, Ruth, and I did not intend to be disrespectful. I am sorry if I upset you in any way."

"Apology accepted." Her acceptance was accompanied by a kiss on the cheek.

After supper well still sitting at the table, Ruth suggested that Arthur inspect Merlin's handy work. "Come, let's have a quick look at the furnace before bedtime. I want to see the loading platform at the chimney top. There should be an opening there to feed the furnace." They mounted the platform. The opening was sealed with a specially made heave brick block. It had bevelled edges and top to fit snugly into an aperture with the corresponding bevelling. She eyed up the platform and chimney. It seemed to meet her approval. "Now, let me check to see if this heavy block we've made for a door can be slid in and out easily when hot."

There was a chain attached to the block to facilitate this operation. Ruth pulled it open. "You'll have no trouble loading the coal and ore through this small door. And when the temperature is right, the sword effigy will also pass through an opening this size. Merlin's done a fine job." She then tried to close the door with the aid of a pushing pole made for this purpose. "This F-ing door's so heavy, but you should be able to handle it much easier than I did. You're much stronger than I am. Just be mindful when closing it to ensure it has a good seal. So make sure there are no bits and bobs in the way." She pointed to the edges. Merlin had come to see if everything had met with Ruth's approval.

"Is the structure satisfactory, Lady Ruth?"

"You and the men have done a wonderful job, Merlin." Arthur then spoke up.

"The only thing Lady Ruth questioned was the door to the f-ing. She said it was heavy."

"What is The f-ing?"

"It is the opening near the top of the chimney. Remember, you spoke of the door saying the f-ing door was too heavy for you to manage, Lady Ruth." Ruth's face went a little red, not realizing the words she'd used. She quickly covered up, knowing they would not understand her meaning.

"I did say it wouldn't be a problem because it would be you working the door."

"This is so, Lady Ruth, but you also did not explain bits and bobs." He just laughed.

"Now, you're really pushing the envelope."

"More strange words Lady Ruth. More strange words." He shook his head and smiled.

The following morning Arthur was sent to work at the rock. Guinevere met up with him there later in the day, carrying a picnic launch. "You must come and sit to take launch with me. If you question my motive, it is because, My Liege, you must maintain your strength. One day you will need that strength to wield that great sword you are making with ease."

Arthur did not need a second request. He dropped the tools he was using to move close to the spot on the grass where she had sat.

"Let us find somewhere a little more private away from prying eyes." They slipped away from the group of spectators that seemed to be ever-present. He enticed her to a lonely spot overlooking the gorge. After picking a grassy comfortable-looking area that appeared to meet their needs, they sat overly close to each other. He quickly took a bite of food a swig of cider before looking into her eyes.

"You are so beautiful, Guinevere, and so hard to resist." The young prince took her in his arms and kissed her. She, in turn, embraced Arthur, then fell back onto the grass. As their embrace became more passionate, it took a much more sexual course. He felt her breasts as he moved on top of her. Her groin moved upwards to press against his. His reaction was swift. Lifting her skirt, he increased her simulation even more with his hand. Things had now gone beyond their control. This relationship's consummation followed. Oh, what an exhilarating experience it had become: Two young lovers, virgins exploring first love together, an act that could only cement a lifelong bond with this experience to be cherished forever.

Their special moment in time was short live. Ruth had unexpectedly appeared. "It would seem there will be another ceremony to take place in the not-to-distant future. And It looks like I will have to be your maid of honour, Guinevere. Because I think you've just lost yours." She started to laugh uncontrollably. They joined in the laughter. "Well, young Arthur, if you have that much energy, let's harness it. Back to work, Arthur, immediately."

With willing hands to load the cart, enough stone chippings had been cleared and collected. This left the slab of rock containing the sword standing out alone. Carefully a crack was opened up by chiselling behind the effigy. It was then supported with a makeshift wooden cradle before finally prying the whole thing free in one peace. Everything was then transported to the furnace. Many followers were joining what had become a procession. As they neared journeys end, Arthur picked up the effigy in his arms and carried it at the front of this rather large band of followers up to the furnace for all to behold. Everything was then ceremoniously placed on the furnaces loading platform and made ready for smelting.

The following day a wax pattern of the sword was scalped. This replica was then placed hilt down and attached to a small wax pedestal. A frame of wood was then placed around this replica, and a slurry of sand and clay was then poured in to form a mould. It was then placed in an oven to dry. The wax ran from this receptacle for the molten steel in this drying process. A tap spout and trough had also been moulded to resemble a sword. This would give a visual effect for the crowd to appreciate. The mould was then upended and placed at the end of the furnace trough. Now all was ready.

After charging it with coal, iron ore, and limestone chippings, Arthur lit the furnace. The water wheel was set in motion, and the bellows began pumping. It took several hours and a few more coal loads before the ore started to melt. It was at this moment in time Ruth poured the alumina powder into the bellows intake. Within minutes the furnace temperature soared. Ruth nodded to Arthur. "Now." as a crowd gathered to watch, he gently fed the sword effigy into the furnace. Ruth then tossed in the medallion.

It was not long before the furnace seemed to radiate its heat.

"Time to break open the tap hole Arthur." He went to the front of the furnace and carried out his orders.

Molten metal ran from its spout. Ruth skimmed off surface dross with a wooden staff as it ran down the open pouring channel before entering the mould. People pointed well, shouting (look, the sword is free from the stone, Arthur must be the King in the prophecy. The excess metal was allowed to run off into open moulds, where it was allowed to form into sheet metal. All there was left to do now was wait for the steel to cool. It was a good time for some refreshment.

* * * * *

Arthur seized the cooling mould and threw it into the small lake that had formed below the water wheel. Ruth waded in, broke open the casing and washed off the remaining sand in her skirt. This also polished this stainless steel sword slightly before presenting it back to Arthur. He then waved it high above his head for all to see. The crowd cheered at the sight of this gleaming sword in the hands of their prince. "Proclaim him King, Proclaim him King." The crowd chanted.

"There must be a Carnation. Let us make ready for such an event," Merlin announced. "It should take place at Glastonbury in the house of Christian worship." This proclamation was met with cheers from the crowd. "One week from today, you must all spread the word of this great event. I will supervise the proceedings. Let us go now to make ready. There will be little time for rest between then and now." The crowd started to slowly disperse to go their separate ways.

Merlin took charge of the sword for tempering before it was honed and polished on sanding wheels powered by the water wheel: With final polishing completed by hand. Merlin had crafted its handle from cheery wood with gold and silver inlays with a magnificent gemstone set into the hilt. This was the crown and glory that achieved its regal elegance. Scrolls carved into its blade made the sword indeed a work of art to behold. As Arthur picked up the finished sword for the first time, Merlin said. "Such a fine sword of a King should have a unique name."

Before anyone else could speak, Ruth shouted, "Excalibur is the sword's name is, Excalibur."

Arthur's reply was as swift as he waved it high over his head.

"Excalibur, a regal name for a King's sword." Merlin cheered.

"Excalibur it is. Without question, it's a fitting name."

CHAPTER 10

The villagers were summoned to attend a formal meeting. Arthur was about to address the meeting when there was a call from a village member. Leo, Guinevere's father, put forward a proposal. "Our new King should have a Queen to reign at his side." This calculated move was a ploy to push his own self-serving agenda. There was an immediate response from Arthur. "For me, that choice has already been made. I have chosen Guinevere to be my Queen. I asked her recently, and she accepted my proposal. I will now ask her again before this gathering of friends for them to bear witness. Will you, Guinevere, accept me as your husband?"

"Yes, I will, Arthur, and I swear, before this gathering of friends, you will always be my one and only love." The people at the meeting were ecstatic. This was everything he and they could have hoped for. This would give him high status in this community, being the father of their soon-to-be Queen. Ruth was not that easily impressed by local politics. She just rolled her eyes at Merlin before smiling and whispering in his ear.

"She could hardly say no, could she; after all, he has already screwed her."

"Ruth, you can be such a bad lady sometimes."

"Yes, and don't you just love me for it." He gave a quick nibble on her ear before pulling away laughing.

Then there were cries from the crowd for a wedding ceremony to be carried out immediately. It was an overwhelming consensus that this should happen within the next few days. Also, it was suggested that the very next day, a time and place should be arraigned. Again Leo was the prime mover to push this agenda. He then put his arms around Arthur, embracing him as the son he'd never had. Another calculated move by Leo to cement this new relationship. He was aware that this opportunity would give him enhanced status to be manipulated for personal gain from this time on. With an arm still around Arthur, he spoke to the crowd.

"I will refurbish and polish the old centurion's armour and plumed helmet for this wedding. Then it can again be worn by our Proclaimed King at his carnation. It will make the perfect regalia for our new Monarch. It will give that appropriate air of dignity well-projecting authority. It should also be worn with a regal cape befitting a King on both auspicious occasions.

Ruth again whispered for Merlin's ears only. "Who would have guessed her father would be such a conniving showboater. Oh well, like father like daughter, I suppose. She knows how to manipulate with the best of them, but I still like her."

"I did not understand half of what you spoke of, but please do not explain. I probably would not wish to know. It would probably be regarded as treasonous with the way you word things." He gave her a reassuring hug. "I ofttimes think your explanations are misconstrued by translation." He then pulled her closer to kiss her lightly on the cheek.

Leo was now fired up and not about to loosen his control of the proceedings. Ladies of the village, who can make such a cape?" There were many offers. It was then unanimously agreed it should be a joint effort. Many hands make light work, and there was little time to waste.

This group of volunteers then left the meeting to commence their labour of love, signifying support of this new allegiance. Arthur was whisked away to enjoy his last nights as a single man. Ruth and Merlin walked back to the cave to spend more quality time together: This was their time. Their part in all the arrangements was now complete. It was up to others to make all the appropriate arraignments for the upcoming events.

The following day the whole village was a hive of activity. The wedding ceremony, planned for that next evening, was the hamlet's focus. It would be an event the likes of which would never ever be seen again. Guinevere was being groomed and pampered by her close friends. This pampering started at daybreak. It was intended to continue until the ceremony was about to begin. Her mother's wedding dress would need to be fitted to her form. A vial of the most delicate white lace was held in place with an interwoven headband of fresh white flowers and greenery. This had to be fitted and ready for its last-minute assembly at that precise moment before the event was to take place. Her long black hair was to be styled and curled to fall around her shoulders. Her bouquet was also in the process of being fashioned to match her headband. There was an addition, supplied by the extra touch of colourful red roses as the peace centre.

Arthur had been kept secluded in a cave near Merlin's cave, where his dress regalia had been delivered. The foundation for this dress was a gold-embroidered white knee-length shirt. It was drawn at the waist with a wide black leather belt: An attachment was added to secure a scabbard. From the belt hung studied straps of leather as thigh protectors. The swards sheath had been specially modified for Excalibur, as it was much broader at the hilt than the Roman short sword it had been initially made for. Excalibur's design differed in several other ways than most swords of that era. Excalibur's long sharp, tapering pointed blade could easily pierce or slash through bronze armour without braking because of the exceptional quality of steel the sword had been fashioned from. Even the early steels now being produced were no match for this finely crafted weapon. Its refashioned scabbard had openings in its front, so the brilliance of its superior craftsmanship could be easily viewed yet still held secure.

Guinevere's father took on the task of an armourer. He assisted with the fitting of body armour and the Plumed helmet. Naturally, last-minute adjustments had to be made before a final polish and before placing Arthur's cape around his shoulders.

Where was the cape? Everyone seemed on edge except Ruth, whose philosophy seemed to be shit happens, but things still seem to work out alright in the end. "The cape has not yet been delivered, and the sun was starting to sink low in the evening sky. It will have to be delivered before nightfall to ensure the fitting did not need alterations." Leo's anxiety, frustration and blood pressure were reaching their limit, as seen in a face that looked ready to explode. His heart lightened as a young woman from the village was seen running towards the cave, carrying the cape. Ruth was taken aback at the sight of this young woman because she was her physical double. She handed Ruth the cloak as their eyes locked in astonishment. They couldn't seem to break their stare until the woman spoke.

"I am, Nimue of Avalon. I'm also the barre of a message. When Arthur rides towards the village tomorrow evening, we will have lookouts on guard so Guinevere can be there to join him. When Guinevere has joined Arthur, they can then ride together through the village."

"Please tell Guinevere we will make sure everything goes as planned.

Before you leave, you must assist me with fitting the cape. We must ensure alterations will not be required. Our soon-to-be King Arthur is fully dressed in his regalia, so a fitting should not take long." The cape was carefully placed around Arthur's shoulders. This red velvet cape trimmed with white fur only enhanced the already regal grandeur explicitly designed to elevate Arthur's appearance to that of an undisputed King.

Leo took it upon himself to make sure the King's regalia was perfect in every way. His interference was starting to get out of hand. Most of his concerns were so trivial that they got to the point of becoming annoying. This excessive fussing took way too much time and started to try Ruth's patience.

"Leo! Nimue needs to leave before nightfall."

"Let me deal with this. Go have a cider with Merlin."

Ruth nodded to Nimue, who then departed to rejoin Guinevere's entourage. Ruth then looked at Merlin.

"Please pour a cider for Arthur and me. I think we both deserve one."

"He must take off his regalia before drinking cider. I do not want a spill tarnishing the armour I have polished so carefully." Now with her back towards Leo, she rolled her eyes at Merlin. He just smiled as he handed her a mug of cider. She changed the subject to ease any stress that might cause a riff.

"Did you see that girl Merlin? I have a double, not just a lookalike, an actual double."

"Even I could not tell the difference between you both. It was uncanny. However, there was something about Nimue that was different. I can not place what it was, but I could tell she was not you and never could be."

The following afternoon became the final dressing before the marriage ceremony was started. Again Leo continued with his overly annoying hindering. What began as a minor annoyance towards this man had slowly turned into anger for Merlin. Ruth could see Merlin's frustration building. In the hope of defusing, what could be an awkward situation, she whispered in Merlin's ear.

"That twit's turning out to be a right royal pain in the ass, isn't he!" Ruth's comment gave a more lighthearted perspective on the man. What was meant to be a snicker as a reply from Merlin turned into a burst of full-blown laughter? For him, this was a healthy release for the frustration he was starting to feel from Leo's overly obsessive behaviour.

"Perhaps it is time for another cider Ruth." She knew exactly what he meant and winked her eye.

Arthur was more interested in his personal preening. He was also intent on pampering the haughty black stallion he'd been presented with. These distractions had consumed his attention, so much Arthur was oblivious to others' antics at this point. This magnificent steed was a gift from the community, and he would be riding it for the first time on this auspicious occasion. Everything was allowed to proceed to the next level only after Leo deemed Arthur's dress was perfect.

With Merlin's assistance and the help of the meddling Leo, Arthur was heaved into the saddle. He then began his ride to the altar. His entourage from the gorge followed behind in an orderly precession. Their planned path would take them to the edge of the village, where Arthur would meet with Guinevere. From there, they would ride together to a holy shrine, an altar of God, where the marriage ceremony would be performed by a priest. This altar was situated on the far side of the village. This would enable all of Arthur's followers who had travelled from outlying areas to line the street to watch the procession pass. This would also allow supporters to show allegiance to their proclaimed King on his wedding day. As he and his future bride proceeded forward to take their vows.

Reaching the main street, they were joined by the bridal procession. Guinevere mount was a white mare making the two horses the perfect pair for this occasion, as were their riders. She rode up alongside Arthur as the two groups merged to continue their journey to the altar. At the ceremonial table of God, they both dismounted with the aid of their entourage. The congregation was called to order, and the ceremony was performed. It was done with all the grandeur befitting the wedding of royalty.

With the Holy ceremony completed, the wedding party moved to a bridle suite specially prepared for Arthur and Guinevere. The bride and groom started to disrobe as they gathered in the room. Only then did It dawn on Ruth the reason they were all here.

In this Now, it was Ruth's duty: With this band of friends and relatives, too witness the consummation of this Royal marriage. 'Oh my God,' she thought, 'I'm about to watch a porn show. Well, at least I won't be staring in it or participating in any way.' Arthur now buck-naked and, on top of Guinevere, started to perform his husbandly duty. Ruth could not help but think with a snicker; Guinevere was lucky to have such a well-endowed husband. There were smiles and nods of approval from the witnesses as the porn show continued. Sounds of pleasure were now coming from the couple. The onlookers showed their appreciation and their seal of approval with a round of applause. The Curtain finally fell on this performance. Witnesses filed from the room. A self-appointed spokesman Leo addressed the crowd outside. Leo held his hands high in the air and shouted, "The marriage is consummated." This brought cheers of joy from the crowd.

The party then moved to the centre of the street, where tables set with food and drink were laid out. The celebrations then continued on almost until the crack of dawn.

CHAPTER 11

People who had not over-indulged in the wedding celebrations the previous evening were now crawling from their sleeping holes. The bright light from the sun, already high in the sky, greeted them. This hardy few then took it upon themselves to fully awaken the remaining wiry bunch of revellers who had also begun to stir. Then began a lot of head rubbing and stretching that seemed to do little for that which ailed them. The only solution appeared to be, and only for the more adventurous, an early morning dip. These gallant few saute stimulation from the cool but inviting stream waters. This seemed as good an option as any to try. Several more daring bodies ran to midstream, where they immersed themselves entirely in those refreshing waters. Others less venturous wadded in more cautiously. There was an abundance of screaming and yelling that accompanied this rude awakening. These full-hardy revellers had chosen a form of stimulation that was definitely more braising than anticipated. Staggering out of the water to dry off in the warmth of the noon sun, these hardy souls then mingled with the less adventurous.

There was little enthusiasm for anything else on that early afternoon other than spending a lazy day recuperating from the previous evening.

Bodies lined the entire street, seemingly incapable of doing anything but relaxing and occasionally socializing with friends and neighbours. However, when Arthur and Guinevere appeared on the scene, there was a renewed sense of focus. Their King and Queen had arrived.

"We must commence our march to Glastonbury tomorrow for my coronation and that of my Queen. I call upon the elders of this community to start this grand event at that time." Plans had been made to start the march at the break of day the very next morning. This command had been expected. Runners were dispatched to spread the word across the south of Britannia of their new King's Coronation. They were to tell how he was destined to be crowned one week from this day at Glastonbury. Preparations already started simultaneously as the wedding was now put into play. Transportation previously assembled for the trip was loaded for an early start the next day. Everything seemed to be going as planned for this event, the weather was favourable, and spirits were high. The community had all agreed upon a long night's rest and a fresh morning's start. The parade to Glastonbury was intended to be a spectacular event. Many banners had been retrieved from storage, and many more had been made, especially for this occasion. This journey, this pageant, would allow it to be a talking point to be passed on to future generations of all the people that viewed it along the way. Indeed a spectacle to be remembered. For this purpose, it was given all the pomp and ceremony befitting this rare occasion: The coronation of a King whose rule would encompass all of Britannia and beyond.

Ruth and Merlin had taken a back seat for these proceedings, and their ride was Guinevere's cart drawn by Carrot the donkey. Although Merlin had cleaned it up somewhat, it was not to Ruth's standards. She went to great lengths decorating it with greenery and flowers to give it that festive air. Ruth had forgotten that she was a person out of step in this Now, but here she was determined to enjoy every experience available to her. As a visitor in this Now, she had learned to identify with it, so thoroughly it was hard to believe this was not her place in time. Ruth was aware deep down inside her time here was nearing its close. Soon it would have to be a sad farewell to these people in this Now she'd come to love. Her affiliation with this period was an association she would always remember and perhaps return to one day.

Every village and small hamlet had turned out to cheer this cavalcade led by Arthur and Guinevere riding on their respective mounts. In his royal regalia, Arthur looked every bit Guinevere's Knight in shining armour and the people's soon-to-be King. Followers along the way had swelled the ranks of this royal procession from hundreds to thousands.

Arriving at Glastonbury, the cavalcade was greeted by another crowd of thousands that had come from afar to witness this monumental event. The news of this coronation had been well received throughout the land. This King would unite all the small parishes into one country and hopefully bring back law and order enjoyed under Roman rule. Safe trade routes could again bring prosperity to what had become a lawless society. Traders and merchants could travel the land under the King's protection. Businesses could once more flourish in this safe environment. Protection from raiders in ships from Saxony praying on coastal communities at will could be challenged with force from a united kingdom. It was a time of prosperity. A prophesied future that made this occasion so crucial to this congregation.

The coronation took place at an open-air altar set up for the occasion. This enabled the whole congregation to view the proceedings. Glastonbury Tore itself was alive with people. Its steep slopes gave an excellent vantage point for spectators. After the ceremony, Arthur spoke to his subjects.

"I will parade my standard around the country for all to see. Then I will choose a sight to build my castle, a place that will serve today's needs. My father's castle, my place of birth, is not strategically placed to serve this purpose. I have consulted with my wife, your Queen, on this matter. She has extensive knowledge of this land. She has suggested a place we have both given much thought to. It is an old Roman stronghold to the north where two rivers join: The Avon River and The Frome River. We'll build bridges over these rivers, toll bridges. This will supply financing for this significant venture. Repairing old roads that have been left to decay will once more become the main thoroughfares they once were. Merchants and traders will travel from all over for commerce without fear of robbery. Whatling street, the old Roman road, leads east directly to London. I will also open up trade routes into Wales and the north. My castle will be a safe place for people to visit to conduct commerce. We will make it a cultural centre for all to enjoy, a destination in its own right. And hopefully, they will return many times. I need a great name, a welcoming word for such a place to visit, a place to come for business rest, and recuperation.

It lies in the longest river's tight cam (or bend). There are several cams in this river. The spot for my castle is where it cams a lot more than the other cams. That is why I will call my castle where all will be welcome, Camealot. Who of you will join me and support me in this endeavour? I will need strong men of good character to make this land a safe and prosperous place to live. We will build an army of skilled fighting men. Knights of the realm to administer our laws. It will be a time of peace and plenty for all." The population gave resounding cheers as Arthur and Guinevere symbolically mounted their horses to lead this procession on Its new quest.

Ruth thought were, 'I've created a politician as well as a King.' She had a private snicker well thinking, 'I wonder who wrote his speech.' Looking at Merlin with a tier in her eye, she said, "I think it's time for me to leave. We must return to the gorge. It's there we must say farewell."

"I knew this time would come, but where will you go from here, my one and only love." These words did not make it easier for her, and she held his hand.

"I'm not sure, but I will never forget you or our time together. You also will be my one and only true love. I know this as fact." It was a slow, quiet journey back to Cheddar, with a lot of touching, snuggling and caressing to fill the void of silence.

Their last night in the cave together made for a much more caring, tender rendition in lovemaking than any previously experienced. This was nearing the final goodbye that was heart-wrenching for both of them. Two lovers, condemned by time to eternal separation. Ruth slipped out of their bed in the morning's early hours and made her way back to the portal. She entered the place with a heavy heart. It was the place she would exit this, Now. Ruth was about to place her hand on the tablet when she was startled by a hand gently touching her shoulder. In the gloom of this crevice and partly distracted by grief, she had not noticed Merlin following close behind. "Merlin, you should not be here."

"I could not let you leave without saying goodbye. But this is a doorway to nowhere you were about to walk into. Is that the key to this door?" He pointed to an identical round stone pad Ruth had been first keyed into by Peter. "I have seen a stone with these markings before at the Henge. My father taught me a sequence of symbols many years ago, saying I would need them one day. It never occurred to me those were the symbols on the stone at the Henge until I saw this stone. Perhaps he did not know their purpose either, but I feel this is the day he spoke of and prepared me for. I did not understand what those symbols represented until now, but these doorways are how you come and go at will. These symbols are some kind of key that will open that door. Am I correct, and is this not fact, Ruth?" She was lost for words. It took some time for her to comprehend the gravity of the situation.

"Where did your father get this knowledge, Merlin."

"It was passed down to him and his fathers before him by the ancients who built our great stone monuments. He said I was to be a chosen one who would do great things. I had thought at first this was perhaps a father's hopes and dreams for his son. However, over time he persisted with this story. He then told me that I would visit other places and times one day. My first task would be to assist in the conception of a child who would be of great importance to our people one day. Also, there would be many other great events I would help shape for this land's good. It would then be my destiny to visit many other exotic places to ensure important events would happen as they are ordained to happen." Ruth's jaw dropped in amazement. This utterly unexpected revelation made his knowledge of the situation a little unnerving.

"Do you know who these ancients were?"

"I was told they were called Gate Keepers, and one day I would meet one who would explain to me the role I was destined to play. Are you that person Ruth?.

"I don't know. I wish I could speak to Peter; perhaps he would explain this situation." There was a pause. "Or maybe not." Her thoughts were, 'Another learning experience for you, Ruth, it will all become clear to you eventually. Yep, this would be his advice. Oh well, here we go. Now how do I explain something I don't understand myself.' "Well, apparently, you seem to have been recruited for some reason or another, just like me. So touch the symbols known to you, place your hand at the centre and off we go through the gate."

"My way is not your way at this time, Ruth. There are things I know I must do alone. Any time we need to be together, we enter a portal and think of each other, and we will be together. Is this not correct."

"How do you know this, Merlin? You seem to know more than I do about the gates. Where did you get this knowledge?"

"As I explained, legends passed down through time from the ancients. This is information that I am only now starting to understand. Perhaps this has always been my destiny, as it also seems to be yours. Again, am I correct in this thinking?"

"That's something you and I can only speculate about, Merlin. So knowing we will meet again, this is not goodby. So until we meet again, I'll let you go first, as it will be your first experience." He kissed her on the cheek, touched the symbols put his hand on the stone and became that being of light before entering the portal to vanish into time and space.

CHAPTER 12

There was something familiar about the museum portal, so she looked back to check more carefully. Yes, it had to be the same one she had just entered in Cheddar Gorge. The gallery was empty, probably due to some mechanism within the system to ensure its secrecy. Her arrival seemed to have been calculated so as not to attract attention. Peter also stepped through directly after Ruth, again unobserved.

"Well again, I walked into a situation I have a feeling you were fully aware of. I know what you're going to say; it's just another learning experience for you, Ruth. Just relax and let it happen. It will all become clear to you soon." Peter smirked.

"You really do know me well, don't you, Ruth."

"Now, this is the same portal that was in Cheddar, is it not."

"You can find the answer to that question by simply asking the exhibit." This she did.

Her suspicions were confirmed as it told how the portal was on lone in an exchange program from another museum. It then displayed a life-size hologram of another find from the same location. It was a perfect reconstruction of her furnace. The explanation that followed astounded

Ruth. It told how this artifact, the furnace, was far more advanced than anything discovered in this ancient period. It explained how it had become a prize exhibit of the British Museum. It had been established beyond doubt from trace residue in its lining; the alloy produced in this furnace was stainless steel of the highest quality. This alloy was believed to have only been invented approximately fifteen hundred years later. Another speculation was the sword Excaliber was a product of this technology.

There was also advanced technology in this new Now Ruth could not even have imagined. It was a technology known as (The Residual Energy Pattern Reconstitution and Display System). This process enabled scientists to transform an energy footprint left by a living entity into an exact holographic image of that being. It then explained it as being much like ghostly apparitions. Such events had been happening naturally throughout time. A phenomenon until this discovery, scientists had no specific explanation for.

It continued its story by saying a cave in this area had been occupied by people who had used this metallurgical technology. Its next hologram showed Ruth, Merlin, Arthur, and Guinevere. Peter Looked at Ruth with a knowing eye.

"My! people in this Now have come a long way. I wonder what will be revealed next? Well, with my lookalike front and centre in this display, perhaps we should move on before someone asks for an autograph." Before she had time to say another word, the museum curator emerged from his office and approached them.

"Greetings, my name is Jordan. I am the curator of this museum. You seem to have set off a few alarm bells in my office. The only explanation I can attribute this to is you are conducting a review of our procedures. If so, how can I be of assistance."

"I am Peter, and this is my companion." There was a brief pause as though in thought before continuing. "Petra." Ruth gave Peter a surprised look, well, keeping it as discreet as possible. At that same moment, Jordan glanced towards the holographic display.

"Oh my, I can see we have a problem here. Our display somehow has developed a malfunction. I see why alarm bells went off in our security system. Somehow it's picked up on your energy signature and integrated it into the display. This is a major problem for a system deemed infallible. Our entire justice system has convicted criminals based on information obtained from the Residual Energy Pattern Reconstruction Display System. As you are well aware, its design was initially developed as a tool to apprehend criminals. You must understand the ramifications of this system failure. It's been the main contributing factor in making our society crime-free for a hundred years and more."

"Perhaps a simple electrical short circuit."

"A simple short circuit, a simple short circuit. Did you not learn anything in school, girl? Perhaps five hundred years ago, a statement like that could have been a valid one, but not with today's technology. Maybe you should consider a reeducation program, or at least have your implants checked. Or perhaps you're one of those individuals that crave extreme external stimulation and, in doing so, have damaged one of your receptors. You've not had your implants removed, have you? I'm not dealing with a Teckout, am I? An assessment would definitely be in order either way. I must contact bioengineering and place it in their hands. Ruth was afraid to ask what a Teckout was as it could prove to be more detrimental than informative. On the other hand, Peter did have some questions of his own.

"If a Teckout could manipulate the system so easily, how secure is it, really? This is why we are here to see if the system could be manipulated. I find it hard to believe our engineers overlooked just how easy it was to compromise the system by using a Teckout in this manner. Petra kindly volunteered to be our guinea pig for this experiment by temporarily removing her implants and becoming a Teckout. And as you see, the system is not infallible. In fact, it failed miserably. Now, whose identities have been assigned to the holograms in this display. Or, more accurately, I should say who have you surmised them to be?" Peter said this with authority to put Jordan on the defensive, implying Jordan was Perter's subordinate to his perceived civic powers.

"Up until now, we had identified them as being Merlin the magician, King Arthur, Guinevere and the Lady of the Lake. Apparently, we thought we had found her to be a person called Lady Ruth." Peter put his hand to his face and gave a chuckle.

'What does Peter know that I don't,' Ruth thought to herself. 'Or was it just coincident he said my name was Petra?'

"Did you not contemplate for one minute the odds against such a coincidence as this. These fore iconic mythical characters being found in one spot at the same time. Would that not be totally improbable? Not without saying, if they did, in fact, actually exist. The chances of such a find would have to be calculated at one in a billion, at least. I think you've been the target of some kind of hoax. Or an attempt to corrupt the system and expose its weakness." At this point, holographic apparitions started to replace the exhibit in the form of what seemed to be an outraged crowd. Nearly all were professing innocence for some wrongdoing they had been accused of perpetrating.

"This did not take long to happen. You've created a nightmare for society by bringing this problem to light in such a public place." Peter took the high road in this conversation.

"If this situation had not been made public, perhaps the ruling council would have dealt with it unicameral, and one can only imagine the outcome of their decision. This dilemma needs to be dealt with in an open public forum. A transparent enquiry for all to see must proceed.

Private enquiries have a habit of taking the line of least resistance and not necessarily the correct path. Would you not agree, Jordan?"

"Your point is a valid one, Peter, and I'm sure you will be asked to become an overseer in the enquiry process."

"I have a busy schedule, as you can well imagine, but I will do my best to accommodate the counsel's wishes on this matter. However, this matter has shed new light on the case of Rouge Monica. A new review of his charges should now be the prime objective of this enquiry."

"As you say, because we have such a large audience, how can this case not be revisited."

It became clear to Ruth Peter knew much more of this period, this Now, than she had been led to believe. 'Oh yes, he is in for some harsh words and a lot of explaining when I get him alone.'

"I would suggest we now visit bioengineering, so Petra, my companion, may have her implants replaced as soon as possible." This request drew dagger-ed looks from Ruth, as Peter had anticipated. He made a discreet sign with his hand and eyes to hush and that all would be well. "We will take our leave of you, for the time being, Jordan, to attend to matters at hand."

"I understand, and I'm sure we will meet again in the not too distant future."

When out of earshot, Ruth set into Peter. "What the hell was that all about. I think you have a lot of explaining to do."

"Yes, I do, this time; you get a full explanation. It's time for you to expand your horizons somewhat. Let's go to the cafeteria and talk over coffee, for there is a lot to explain. And I think now is the time some secrets can be safely reviled. You've accepted so much and learned so much more. What I'm about to tell you should not come as such a shock." They ordered coffee and found a secluded place to sit where their conversation could be conducted in complete privacy.

"As you've already deduced, I'm familiar with this place. There is a critical point in this Now that we have addressed. This is not my Now of origin, as you may also have guessed." Ruth interrupted.

"Are you one of the ancients I've heard so much about in my travels?"

"Yes and no."

"Great, tell all in riddles. How could I have expected anything different from you."

"Please, Ruth, it's not like that. Which came first, the chicken or the egg? That is the Dilemma here. You see, my own Now of origin is thousands of years on from this Now. However, my people established colonies on earth at the dawn of mankind to create our species. We designed ourselves to be precisely how we are. Mankind is the product of our own creation."

"Woe! Are you saying your people collectively are God?"

"Well, I wouldn't go that far, but you get the picture. You also see how important it is that the timeline of the Now's will develop as ordained or our society would crumble."

"You picked me for what? Where do I fit into this picture? I'm no superhero set to save the world."

"I've not been completely celibate all my life, Ruth. You see, I do have a lover, my wife, and a child. My wife, her Now, has been completed, and she resides in the universe of light. I visit her there often, and I will join her there one day when I retire." Peter reached his hand across the table and placed it on Ruth's. "My wife, the love of my life, was named Naomi."

"But that was my mother's name."

"Yes, that it is. We named you Ruth when you were born. As you now know, my life is unconventional by your standards, to say the least. The inability to age would have been a problem eventually. It was decided your mother should raise you alone as a normal child. One day, it was also agreed that you would be told the whole truth about who you really are. Today is that day. The name Petra is the title my mother used. She suggested that it could also be used in conjunction with your name one day: That would be if you so wished. Our customs differ slightly from those of your Now of origin." This was all too much for Ruth to absorb. The emotion at this moment was just too extreme. She tried to hold it together but could not control the tears erupting from her eyes. She got up from the table to leave. Peter moved around from where he was sitting to comfort her. At first, this all seemed so strange to her. However, a hug from her dad, a father she did not know she had, made it all feel so good. She nestled in his arms, well her tears subsided.

"Now settle yourself down, and we will talk more. You must have many questions requiring straight answers. This time I will do my best to be as honest with you as possible." She thought for a moment.

"I'm sorry this is all a bit too much for me right now. I need some time to think."

"That's fine, take all the time you need. Time is something we always have plenty of." They sat there in silence for a while. Ruth stared long and hard into her coffee cup as though she might find some rational explanation for her predicament there.

"I now understand why you chose me, but why did you not do the same for my mother."

"Your body has certain physical adaptations only evolution could provide. You acquired those properties from my gens. These were properties your mother's body did not possess."

"But Merlin had no such connection to our people. How was he able to use the gate without any harm coming to him."

"Merlin can be only explained as an anomaly, a freak of nature. Perhaps he was the very first human to possess the same genome as my people. It was not the correct time for that gen to be spread throughout society. So as you now know, you averted that happening. You have also chosen a partner that physically is your equal. We all need someone in our lives to fit the bill of lover, confidant, and friend. In Merlin, I think you've found that person. Now perhaps a wedding is in order. If so, I would be so proud to give the bride away." This comment was accompanied by a broad smile. She slapped his hand.

"Oh, Dad, Dad, that has a nice ring to it. I like it. It sounds much less formal than Mr. Peter Gates."

"That's not my name. That's a nickname you gave me."

"Yes, and you also told me Peter was more of a title than your real name."

"My given name is Jerome." Ruth's laugh brought a skoal to Peter's face.

"Oh, come on, who would name their kid Jerome. No, wonder you tell everyone your name's Peter. I can't call you Dad, you don't look old enough to be my dad, so I'll just carry on calling you Peter. So that's settled Peter Peter, the pearly gates keeper. Now how are we going to slip away from this Now? Someone will be expecting me in bioengineering, so we'll definitely be missed when we leave."

"Just go there, and I will accompany you. The procedure these people wish to perform will not harm you; it will awaken the power within you and speed up your learning process. It will make you aware of your full potential. You have gifts incredible gifts. This was also another reason we came here, so don't be afraid."

"Well, this again is another curveball you've thrown at me, so excuse me for being just a little apprehensive about this procedure."

"It'll be just fine; there's no need to worry. It's a straightforward procedure for people of this Now, and for you, it will be so much simpler. With your gens, this process will be little more than stimulation. You will only require the stimulation, and no implants will be required. This will then give you what you would have only perceived before this awakening as god-like powers. When you visit ancient Greece or Rome, they will take you to be a god. In fact, I'm sure there's a statue dedicated to you somewhere in antiquity."

"You've got to be joking."

"I may have a habit of talking in riddles on occasion, but I seldom joke about serious matters. This will be an enormous change in your life. A coming of age, so to speak. With these new powers come great responsibility, one I now feel confident you are ready to handle."

"I don't know if I should be excited or scared stiff."

"Perhaps both of those emotions are completely in order at a time like this."

"There is one thing that's just occurred to me. Will Merlin need this awakening at some point in time?"

"Merlin's needs must be assessed by you, and when the time comes to broaden his perspective, you may need to bring him to a place like this. Although things have a habit of working themselves out to accommodate such needs. Your awakening could be inspiration enough to influence and instigate all the stimulation he requires."

"Don't tell me, I know. It'll be another learning experience for me." He laughed.

"Come, it's time to visit bioengineering. I'll be with you all the time, so don't be nervous."

It was a simple procedure, much like an x-ray. Peter insisted he should do this procedure himself, circumventing the need for anyone to observe. Thus enabling him to keep Ruth's exact physical attributes secret.

"Well, where to next young lady. Perhaps a holiday would be in order."

CHAPTER 13

I n Aw, she viewed her new surroundings, "Is this where I think it is, Peter?"

"It most certainly is Ruth. Petra, where else would an archeologist choose for a holiday but an archaeological wonder." They'd exited a portal inside one of the rooms inside one of the first main monuments built at Petra. Sunlight streaming through the opening of this chamber illuminated their surrounding with a rose collared hue. Ruth hazarded a guess of their new whereabouts based on the assumption this chamber's unique reddish sculptured rock could only be, in her opinion, that place.

"I wonder which Now we're in. Have you any idea?"

"Perhaps if we were to go outside, we may find clues to that question." The road was crowded with people herding pack animals such as camels and donkeys, all laden with trade goods. All were heading towards the newer city centre relocated down the road away. They joined the caravan to what was determined to be a central weigh station on this trade route. This was a place to find water and rest for weary animals and travellers alike. "I would think we are in a late Nabataean or early Roman Now when Petra was in its full glory. Look far to the right; there's a Roman soldier. By his presence, I would assume this, Now, is a period when Petra was part of the Roman empire."

"Yes, I see. So I think we can safely assume this, Now is some time in the second or third century. I thought of the name Petra. You told me it was my grandmother's name when we entered the portal, and I suppose that brought us here. Peter means rock in Greek, and Petra is the feminine of Peter. That makes you Rock Portal Keeper, and that name would also apply to Petra. That's what you meant when you said Peter was more of a title than your name. I'm guessing Petra was not my grandmother's given name either. So are you going to tell me what her name really is?"

"Ah, well, that's another shock you should brace yourself for. You would know her real name to be Athena, as in ancient Greek Athena."

"Ah, now this can't be true because we all know she was the virgin goddess of wisdom, courage, civilization, and the list goes on. Now the underlying tale is she was a virgin, no son, no daughter and definitely no granddaughter, no descendants period."

"Well, if you believe hearsay and distorted tales past down through time, there's no point in me trying to explain, is there. However, I will tell you this, your grandmother probably was still a virgin in ancient Greece. A lot can happen in three thousand years and more."

"Oh, I'm sorry I was rude. I didn't mean to hurt your feelings, but it is a lot for me to digest right now. Let me think about this for a while, and we'll come back to this conversation later. So, are you good with that?" He smiled and gave her hand a squeeze, then put his arm around her shoulder and gave a gentle hug. As they came closer to where the soldier stood, she recognized his familiar form.

She looked at Peter. "That roman soldier looks like Merlin." Her mood lightened at the thought of seeing Merlin so soon. At that very moment, he waved to her, confirming it was him.

"Ruth, I've been looking all over for you," He shouted. Then putting his arms around her, he greeted her with a kiss. "I knew you had to be here somewhere. And Peter, it's also good to see you again." This greeting was given as a second thought. As his attention was totally consumed by Ruth's presence, he'd barely noticed Peter. He then placed his hands on Peter's upper arms and gave them a firm squeeze, followed by a hearty slap to the shoulders. Peter reciprocated the greeting. "It's been a long time, Peter, but like Ruth, you haven't changed one bit. Now can you tell me where we are because I've never seen such a wondrous place as this before?"

"As for your question, where are we? This place is Petra. It's the main respite for traders on passage to and from their destinations. It's a place far to the east and months of travel by ship from Britain. It's near the northeast end of the Mediterranean sea.

Ruth's told me what a handsome man you've become since our last meeting. Now there's something you should know, a secret I only reviled to Ruth recently. She knew nothing of this when you last met. Ruth is my daughter. And I know things have changed between the two of you since you're no longer that youth we first met in Britain. So my man, as a father, you can imagine I'll be watching you, very carefully, I might add." He gave Merlin a knowing smile as he touched an extended index finger to the side of his nose.

"How can you be Ruth's father? You look younger than I. And if so, why were we not told this before?"

"Well, there's a lot of knowledge out there for you and Ruth to absorb. For the time being, just accept some things as fact until you fully understand all the universe's secrets.

"What is this universe, a library of a sort?"

"The universe! hm. It's the world around us, the stars, the heavens, and so much more. As I've stated, you both have much to learn. This is a great place for both of you to expand your knowledge. You've been told all your life you were a chosen one, Merlin. You are the first of our kind. Both you and Ruth."

"How can that be if you are Ruth's father? You would surely precede both of us because you did say our kind is that not correct."

"I am what you know to be as one of the ancients. However, I have travelled from the future to go to the past. As I mentioned to Ruth, which came first, the chicken or the egg. And as I previously said, there's much for you to learn. Just accept things for what they are, and it will all become clear to you in time. When that moment arrives, you will be able to expand your abilities much the same as Ruth is on the threshold of doing today."

"Ruth, you can explore your newfound powers here without fear of repercussions. The strong belief in numerous deities in this time and place is extensive. If anyone observes you using your new attributes, they will readily accept you as a goddess. Instead of putting you in any kind of danger, that status will protect you. You may have trouble controlling these new powers at first, as most are linked to your emotions. However, you'll soon master that link, and then you'll be able to use them at your discretion.

Merlin, there's so much for you to accept and here is an excellent place to start that adjustment. There are things in this universe that you can't even begin to contemplate yet. This place for you is an insight into something different yet not so different as to overwhelm you. Yes, this is an excellent place to enjoy and learn in. I'll leave you two to your own devices. I must go and greet some old friends. We'll meet up again in another Now of your choosing." Peter walked back down the road towards the portal they had entered the city by.

Ruth and Merlin headed for a small marketplace by walking in the opposite direction to Peter. This would be a place where food, water and trade goods could be bartered for and exchanged.

"This truly is a wondrous place, Ruth. Man-made cave hued from solid rose collard rock with lavishly decorated facades. It also seems to be devoid of vegetation, which to me, is strange. This is so different from my cave in Cheddar Gorge."

"As Peter said, this will open our minds to accept many other different times and places readily. We'll undoubtedly visit many more strange and wondrous places in this new existence we seem destined to be a part of. Although I don't know what's in store for me in this latest excursion." She'd barely finished that sentence when a band of ten or twelve heavily armed raiders stormed into the marketplace. Wooden stalls covered by fringed fabric sun shades laden with merchandise were systematically overturned as they ran a-muck through the market. 'Nabataean Rebels' were the cries shouted by many vendors as they fled for cover. This band of marauders then focused their attention on Merlin because of his Roman centurion dress.

Charging straight towards him with swords drawn, they were undoubtedly about to make an example of this foreign oppressor. The very symbol of the oppression they were rebelling against was there in front of them and vulnerable. Merlin placed himself in front of Ruth and drew his sword to protect her. The blade began to glow as Merlin's energy was channelled through it. This was a new, unexpected and quite alien experience for him, but as the heat from it was felt by his foes, it held their attention for a moment. By then, Ruth's initial fear had also quickly turned to anger. This anger awakened a new ability within. Subconsciously it automatically channelled one of her unique attributes. This metamorphosis would enable her to control this situation by instilling fear in their would-be assailants. This subconscious reflex manifested itself with a radical physical change. Her body immediately transformed itself into one that at least doubled her usual height and size.

This size came with matching proportional strength. With one hand, she righted one of the upturned stalls. This impressive show of force deterred any more aggression from these intruders that had now surrounded them. With his back to Ruth, Merlin had not witnessed this metamorphism. His foes, on the other hand, shook with fear at this perceived deity that now towered before them. Some ran, some dropped their weapons and fell to their knees in reverence to this goddess standing before them. The threat under control, she quickly reverted back to her original size. All this before Merlin had time to notice what had happened. He strutted around, waving his sword like it was he who had won the day single-handedly. He was utterly oblivious to Ruth's role in this escapade as she gave a stern glare towards the vanquished. With a sweep of her hand, she ordered the remaining trouble makers dismissed. They backed away on bended knees, well continually bowing in reverence. This submissiveness totally confused Merlin, having only witnessed the entire episode from his viewpoint.

They continued their stroll through the market and helped set things straight where possible as they passed each stall. Many of the vendors offered up food in reverence and as a sign of appreciation. Accepting some of these gifts, they continued their walk along the main road, which meandered through a narrow cleft in the mountain. "Peter was right in his assumption of what could happen to me."

"What did happen to you, Ruth? Everyone here is in awe of you. What did you do?"

"I think you had to see it to believe it. Everyone looked so small. People seemed to be only the size of small children to me. It's definitely something I can't explain. I picked up a stall with one hand. It seemed so light."

"My sword also drew power from within my being that emitted heat and light. This is all very strange.

We have reached the edge of town, and the gorge has narrowed. There seems to be little else ahead that would interest us. Perhaps we should turn back." At that moment, sounds from above caught Ruth's attention. Sounds too faint for the average ear. Looking up, she saw two of the trouble makers high above on the clifftop prying loose stones. As they loosened, they dislodged rocks. As these rocks started to fall, they dislodged boulders creating a minor landslide. Merchants with pack animals had also entered this narrow cleft on their way out of town. This new assault put this group of travellers in eminent endanger. Merlin turned to wave this small caravan back from this catastrophe that was about to happen. At the same time, Ruth raised her hand to the sky in the falling rocks' direction. The light emanating from the palm of her hand engulfed the falling debris freezing it in time. The stones then reversed their trajectory, showering back towards the two rebels who had initially run away. These two individuals, who had apparently not taken defeat lightly, had mustered up some newfound courage to continue their previously aborted attack. Merlin and the whole caravan party witnessed this supernatural feat performed by Ruth. She looked surprised by the attention she was getting. Although it was not now as unexpected as the first time in the market.

This new catastrophe averted, she joined Merlin, and together hand in hand, they walked back past the caravan towards the city. People in this convey bowed in reverence to this perceived deity who had just delivered them from certain death.

That evening was spent at a campsite amongst new friends, although Ruth still felt uncomfortable in her new role as a goddess. All this bowing and scraping made her ill at ease. She just wanted to be one of the gang. This new status was something quite alien to everything she'd been brought up to believe in.

The following morning breakfast was served to them. It was delivered in a manner befitting their new status of gods. This was an honour, and protocol demanded they should accept it graciously. Enjoying this lavish spread laid before them was an easy task. The women who had prepared this breakfast feast then hovered around them, trying to anticipate and accommodate their every whim. After giving approval and gratitude for this gift and service, Ruth and Merlin were set to embark on a day of exploration.

CHAPTER 14

There was some talk over the breakfast table of a camel race that was to take place in the desert that afternoon. Merlin and Ruth had decided to attend and see what all the excitement was about for themselves.

"I've seen horse racing many times, and I know how that can get the heart pumping, so I assume camel racing can have that same effect."

"I have no idea what a horse race is, and until yesterday I'd never seen or heard of a camel. Yet here we are, and there the camels are." He made a sweeping gesture towards a herd of camels corralled together. "So I think I can safely say it will definitely be a new experience for me. Can you explain a horse race to me to give me some idea of what I might expect?"

"Well, each horse has a rider, called a jockey. The race begins with horses and riders positioned in a straight line across the track. They race down the track to the preset finish line as soon as the start signal is given. The one that crosses that line first is the winner."

Those rules sound simple to follow. It seems like a fun spectacle to behold. I wonder how fast they can run; they look quite ungainly to me."

"Don't be misled by appearances. I've heard they run very fast. No doubt, there will be someone making book on the outcome."

"Books are mostly made by monks or scribes. I see neither here. What is the connection between making books and camel racing? Does every race have a tale of its own to be told so people can read and relive the experience at a later time? Or is this book a ledger that recorded all winners of every race run for all to view? " Ruth gave a snigger.

"I'm sorry, it's just a turn of a phrase, common in my Now. It means someone is willing to take a wager on the race's outcome. However, that last analogy of yours is also used in my Now, and it's called a racing form."

"I see. Do you have collateral to engage in such an endeavour for us?"

"If you're asking me if I have money to make a bet on one of the camels, the answer is yes. I seem to have been supplied with some as I came through the gate. Don't you have any?"

"I'll check. I do seem to have a purse tied to my belt." Untying it, he looked inside. "I have roman coins. I wonder if they will be accepted."

"I have the same. Petra is under Roman rule now, so this is probably their legal tender other than gold. Anyhow, I don't think there's anyone here who would have a problem with anything we say or do. Were gods remember." She gave a little chuckle.

Wandering out into the desert towards the crowd who had gathered, they headed towards the area owners were parading their camels. All were saddled, with riders perched towards the rear of each animal.

"It seems to me there are several things to take into account before placing a bet. A healthy, strong lean animal is high on my list. A fit jockey, light in weight, has an air of confidence about him and has that aggressive look. If we choose that right combination, I think we stand a good chance of backing the winner."

"Ruth, are you sure you've never seen a camel race before. For an amateur who claims it's her first time, you seem to be well educated in all the facts surrounding the sport."

"Just a few educated guesses. I don't believe in complete uncertainties. I think that a group of men over there are making wagers. Which is your favourite to win, Merlin?"

"I think I would choose the one with the red embroidered saddle. What is your choice? "

"The same as yours, apparently. I'll give you some of my coins, and you can go place our wager. Even if I am a goddess to those men, it would still not be appropriate for me to interact with them on that basis."

"This is not at all what I'm accustomed to either. Women in this society do seem to be very subservient to men. It is a pity we could not bring Guinevere here for a visit. That should be a revelation for all of these men to dwell upon." Ruth burst out laughing.

"I've never ever heard you make a joke. I was beginning to think you didn't have a sense of humour, but I find that really funny. You'd better go make our bet. I'll walk to the starting line marked out in the sand and wait for you there."

Waiting for the race to start, there was time for small talk. "I've been trying that thing you did with your hands, but all I seemed to have accomplished was to make a tiny black hole appear. No light. I could not make light like you did."

"You made a black hole; that's amazing. What happened next?"

"Objects started to move towards the small black dot, and then I could not seem to control my concentration, and it disappeared. I tried to do it one more time, but nothing happened on that second attempt."

"Perhaps that's just as well for the present time. What you've described is an extremely unpredictable phenomenon. A black hole could drag everything around it in."

"How can that be? Some of the things that moved were too large to go into such a small hole. In fact, everything that moved was too big to fit into that hole."

"A black hole has enormous power, the power of the universe. It's enough energy to crush any object into something so small as not to be seen with the naked eye. Treat this ability with great caution, for goodness sake, or there may be dire consequences. I was given to understand you weren't supposed to have that kind of power until you've undergone the same mind-expanding procedure as I had. It's an opening of the mind to enhance your natural abilities. Perhaps when the race is over, and everyone's left, we can explore our powers in the privacy of the empty desert. It'll be fun to see what else we can do, and with no one around, there should be no risk of collateral damage."

"Collateral damage, what does that mean?"

"The chance of us hurting anyone or thing accidentally. After all, we have no idea what extent these newfound abilities are capable of. Look, I think the race is about to start." The riders were manoeuvring their mounts into position. A flag was quickly waved when the time was right, and all were at the line together. The race began in a swirl of dust. This minor sand storm was created by hooves of racing camels, kicking desert sand high into the air. This sudden spurt of acceleration was encouraged by the crack of the jockey's riding crops on the camel's rumps. Ruth was jumping up and down like an excited young child. Everything personifying that air of dignity befitting the deity she'd been portraying was lost at the drop of a flag.

Merlin quickly lost his more usual surly manner. He was now showing an unusual display of exuberance as their chosen camel took the lead. Ruth and Merlin rejoiced at their perceived win as their favoured stead reached the marker at the far end of the course. Jockeys, however, quickly turned their mounts around at this marker. This was just the first leg of the race. They now had to retrace their path in this second leg of the race. Neither Ruth nor Merlin had realized the start line also doubled as the finish line. Their celebration had been premature. This now made the sport more intense as stomachs churned with anxiety at the thought of having victory snatched from their grasp by this misunderstanding. Competition in this field of play then became more intense as riders and mounts jockeyed for position in the race's last leg.

Another factor that Ruth had not considered in her initial equation was now coming into play. Several of the jockeys worked as a team in this vast field of competitors. Ruth and Merlin's choice still seemed to be the fastest combination of rider and mount in this race. However, this would-be team of competitors working together only accounted for a smaller number of the total field members. Several of this team's members seemed totally intent on outmanoeuvring Red saddle off his path of choice. This strategy then allowed another animal in their consortium a shorter run to the finish line. As the finish line loomed closer, Red saddle made his move. It was a daring one.

A hard push to the flanks of one of his would-be spoilers left enough room for this gallant mount to show its superior turn of speed. It was a stunning finish, enough to stop the bravest heart, but they'd won their bet. Merlin lifted Ruth off her feet swings her around in a victory celebration. This released all the pent-up anxieties accumulated during the race in one gush of exuberance. She kissed him for this show of emotion, an emotion she was revelling in. The sweet smell of success soon vanished when they looked to claim their winnings. The bookie had absconded with their money. After the initial sense of anger had subsided, they looked at each other and laughed. They'd never considered the fact that any payment for them would be a useless commodity in this place and time. There was little here to spend an excess of it on except food and shelter, which seemed to be offered freely anyway. However, the wager did add excitement to the occasion. The thrill of that last moment would be a cherished and long-lasting gift.

Spectators and competitors alike had left the field except for the last few stragglers who were also making their own preparations to go. These people seemed to be the organizers of the race and were discussing the merits of their labours. As with all such events, it needed planning to make it enjoyable and successful. Planing is undoubtedly helped by experience. Experience, in this case, was being developed by the analysis of this event. This information could then be stored in memory and ready for use in their next endeavour.

The desert was now theirs, and it was time for fun. Ruth raised her hands' palms to the sky, and a vortex appeared some forty feet above her. She moved the miny tornado around with slight hand movements. Desert sand was then sucked from the ground by this spinning air mass, which acted like a drill bit boring holes downwards at her command.

"Woe, look at that Merlin, let's see what you can do." She looked around, but Merlin was not there. "What have I done?" There was anxiety in this statement. Was his disappearance something she was responsible for?

"It's alright, Ruth. I'm over here." She could hear him but could not see him.

"Where are you, Merlin? You're making me nervous. Please, what are you doing?" He then appeared ten feet to her left.

"I disappeared from the face of the earth. You could not see me. Perhaps I truly am a magician. This is true wizardry."

"Not so fast, cowboy. It would seem you have the ability to bend light around yourself, giving the illusion that you had vanished. So, what else can you do." He raised his hand in an attempt to recreate the black hole effect. The dust storm created by Ruth's whirlwind was bothering Merlin's eyes and nose. His solution, suck it up like a vacuum cleaner with the void he'd conquered up. He was now having fun with this newly discovered ability moving the black hole around chasing the small sand storm until it had all been completely ingested.

"There, it's your turn next. Ruth, have you any idea what else you may be able to achieve." She pushed her palms downwards and started to levitate. She rose some twenty to thirty feet into the air.

"That is impressive. I will now see if I can achieve that same feat." As his concentration focused on the task, it became almost obsessive so much so it proved to be overkill. Suddenly he shot into the air like a rocket shooting past Ruth fast enough to cause her some turbulence. She then settled herself gently to the ground.

"Whatever you do, don't come down as fast as you went up, or you seriously hurt yourself." Slowly he made a light touch down. "I'm not sure what else we can do, but our abilities seem to be only limited by our own imaginations. I think we've had enough fun for today, so let's make our way back to Petra. What do you think?" On their walk back to Petra, they didn't speak of these new abilities acting as though nothing unusual had happened. However, Merlin was again confused by Ruth's phraseology.

"Why did you ask what I was thinking? Was it just more of your strange talk, or do you wish me to divulge all my secret inner thoughts to you?" She gave a slight giggle.

"I meant I was just asking for your input on my statement."

"You confuse me. Why do you not just say what you mean instead of using this strange talk I can not understand."

"I'm sorry, it's just the way we speak in my Now of origin: We use metaphoric sayings extensively to make a point. We will visit my Now soon. It will be an excellent learning process for you. I'm sure you would enjoy seeing how your world has evolved over time. We could visit the Gorge and look for Camelot and so much more."

"The place where Camelot stood has it long been forgotten."

"Names have a way of changing over time. Bristol is built at the rivers Avon and Frome's meeting place you spoke of. This could be a possible site for Camelot. As we understand, Bristol is derived from a similar Saxon word that transformed itself into Bristol over time, and a bridge over the river is a major thoroughfare. So, it seems Arthur's vision may have come true if all this you've stated ever becomes fact and not just our speculation."

The city of Petra welcomed them back with open arms as they walked the main street. Set inside a large tent, a thick Persian carpet and pillows were offered as logins for the night. Food was again presented as offerings to these perceived gods. It would have been deemed impolite to refuse such gifts, so they were graciously accepted. Retiring to these lavish quarters, they lounged in comfort well, enjoying an exotic spread of food. These foods were totally alien to Merlin. Dates, olives, dried salted fish from the sea, bread with garum fish sauce, and so much more. This was indeed a feast fit for the gods that had been presented exclusively for their enjoyment.

Laying down together, it was time to finish this perfect day with some healthy lovemaking. Ruth's hands caressed his body as he pulled her ever closer, aroused by her stimulation to that part of his body she craved. Merlin massaged her thighs slowly at first. It then became more intense and faster as hearts started to race. He moved his fingers to enjoy that moist, more intimate part of her body. They were now both fully aroused. Accepting him into her, they embrace this saga's next stage that they had played so many times before. Initially, starting this phase of lovemaking was a furious engagement followed by a lull before entering the next steps in this love tango. With the slow, steady rhythm of pleasure upon them,

Ruth pressed her palms to the carpet as she pushed herself up and down to enhance his rhythm. The ground beneath the carpet now seemed much softer than before. It was almost as if they were floating on air. As Merlin pushed, they also seemed to have moved forward. With surprise, they both noticed the tent opening was now behind them. This brought an abrupt end to their lovemaking. Ruth's palms pushing down with uncontrolled emotion had elevated their lovemaking to new highs figuratively and literally. Well, Merlin's pushing had provided forward momentum. By the time they had disengaged and modesty had prevailed, the carpet was some twenty feet in the air and still moving forward at some speed.

"Well, I'm becoming aware that moments like these are what myths and legends are made of." She started to laugh uncontrollably. Merlin joined her in this moment of unfettered humour. "Until this moment, I've always thought it was a farfetched tale. Flying carpets! We have an audience, and I'm sure this story will be told over and over again. It's a legend in the making." Again she could not control her laughter. "I couldn't face going back there again, so let's fly this thing back to the gate."

"Most definitely, I totally agree with you, Ruth. We did make quite a spectacle of ourselves, did we not." This was also a new learning experience, manipulating a carpet to act in such an unusual way. It became a fun chore. By the time they'd landed at their destination, they had both mastered the art of maneuverings this unique flying device.

"We should send this carpet back to its owner. With the story that goes along with it, he could become a wealthy man." She paused then made a point of saying, 'with a smirk on her face.' "What do you think, Merlin?" This time he did not take the bate but simply smiled knowingly. He then made his next statement.

"Events were developing in Britannia when I left I have a feeling I should be a part of. I also think it is something I am destined to do alone.

Since I saw you there last, I met with King Uther Pendragon in his Now. He enlisted my aid in a deception I disapproved of but felt obligated to supply. Giving him my assistance was paramount in Arthur's birth. Without this help, Arthur may not have been born. When Arthur was of age, I requested that he seek me out as his counsel. This he agreed to on the condition I would always serve his heir faithfully. I swore him an oath to that effect. I then returned to Arthur's Now and aided in constructing what you now call Camelot. For many years Camelot prospered. I had many personal adventures in that Now. I travelled through many different periods in Arthur's life by utilizing the portal. Camelot was a gleaming light in society, a place of beauty for all to admire and behold. However, in Arthur's later years, things were not going well for Arthur. Without an heir, he had lost focus. He rejected my advice in favour of counsel from others seeking power for their own personal gain. These subversive policies were for control over his domain, with no regard for his kingdom's good and well-being.

His knights were losing respect for him. Guinevere was accused of undermining his authority with alleged nefarious affairs. The kingdom was again reverting to the shambles it had been when he first took power. Some time has passed since these developments manifested themselves. I feel the need to go back and try to reverse the course of events that put the kingdom in this state of affairs."

"I'm sure you do have unfinished business there. I, too, have some unfinished business in my Now. I feel we will meet again, perhaps in my Now. For you, it will be some future, Now's location. It'll be an excellent experience for you to observe how things change over time. You'll be able to learn a lot from that experience." After Merlin entered the portal, Ruth stepped through the gate. She was fully aware of their different destinations.

CHAPTER 15

On his return to the Gorge, Merlin was saddened to see the cave, the one he'd made his cherished home ransacked and looted over time. Manuscripts relating to his knowledge of nature, engineering, and potions had been stolen. This was his life's work in this Now. It was all gone, erased for history. There was little left for him there, so he hastened to the village to meet with old friends. He was also aware this now was some twenty years past his last visit. He'd not travelled far before he met a young man at the junction leading to the village. The young man greeted him by inquiring about his well-being. "I am well. I am Merlin, but perhaps you are too young to remember me, and you, sir?"

"My name is John, and I have heard tales of Merlin, the magician, but he would be a much older man than you." It was easier for Merlin to tell a lie than explain the truth at this point.

"You then must also know I am a great magician, one that time has no boundaries to constrain or control. I need to speak to Leo. Where might I find him."

"I am sorry to be the bearer of bad news, but he has been dead some ten years past or more. The Lady of the lake, Lady Nimue of Avalon, speaks of you often. She left here to visit King Arthur at Camalot, not but one day past. Since you left all those years past, she has become a valued adviser to the king, second only to Mordred. People in these parts said it was a sad day when you left so many years ago. There will be rejoicing when they hear of your return."

"I fear my stay here will be a short one. It would seem I should make great haste for Camalot, so I bid you farewell, my young friend." Without thought of provisions, he headed back up the gorge towards Camalot some thirty miles north. He did not have the entourage he expected Ruth's imposter to be travelling with and hoped to intercept her before she reached the castle. Merlin barely remembered Ruth's lookalike on Arthur's wedding day, but he vaguely recalled the name. She had to be this imposter, for who else could it possibly be.

The road north was in poor condition showing signs of structural failure from lack of maintenance. However, with iron-willed determination, he was able to make good time. The entourage came into sight at the same moment he glimpsed Camalot's high white stone escarpments in the distance. Even the gleaming white lime wash that once made this castle shine like a bright beacon over its green landscape had also been neglected and now reflected a somewhat shabby rundown look. There was no way to catch the imposter before she entered the castle. They had already crossed the Avon river bridge, and only the main gate and wall stood between them and the Keep. He'd tried so hard to make this happen, but victory in this race against time seemed hopeless and way beyond his grasp. The track he'd been running now seemed to have been an impossible task that he'd set himself. The use of his new powers, the black hole, yes, this could snatch victory from defeat. He focused all his attention on a point on the road. It was an area just ahead of the entourage, and he raised his hand. As power flowed through his body, the black hole started to appear, sucking the roadway into it to form a deep crater directly in front of them.

Horses reared in fright, and guards became disoriented. He then abruptly stopped the flow of power. This gave him a shot of rejuvenated vigour, and a quick sprint across the bridge was all it took to join Nimue's entourage.

"Do you remember me, Lady Nimue of Avalon? I am the magician, Merlin." He emphasized that he was a great magician by levitating high into the air. He then slowly descended back to the ground. Please do not try to convince me you are the Lady of the Lake, for we both know that's not to be true. Your council to the king has been nothing less than self-serving for short-term personal gain. This corrupt advice must stop immediately as it has put the kingdom itself in a dire state. I intend to make that fact quite clear to King Arthur himself in my stay here. So turn your ragtag group of villeins around and go back from whence you came. I swore an oath to his father, King Uther Pendragon, to be Arthur's loyal adviser. This oath I intend to keep."

He had barely finished his ultimatum when an archer appeared from behind one of the wagons. He let loose an arrow. Merlin's reaction was sharp. He grabbed the shaft in flight as if it was standing still. The Archer looked on in terror, fearing the retribution about to take place, but Merlin had vanished from sight. On reappearing, he gave a swiping motion with the back of his hand. This would-be assassin was then tossed into the pit with all the force of a direct blow. Nimue bowed to Merlin in reverence. She accepted his ultimatum after witnessing his power's fury firsthand. Her entourage slowly turned around to make their way back from whence they had come with a promise never to return to Camalot.

This first part of Merlin's task had been completed. Phase two was about to start; this would be to rid the castle of Mordred. He was determined this quest would be accomplished with the same efficiency as the first task he had set himself. When he reached the castle wall, the draw bridge had been raised. Guards had been stationed on the ramparts above. This did not present a problem for an angry Merlin. Leaping into the air and levitating himself even higher, he landed back down on the ramparts. Pushing aside guards that would have sooner welcomed him than opposed him, he made his way to the Keep. Mordred, summoned by his men in time to witness much of what had happened, had no wish to engage in conflict with this powerful magician. He made a hasty retreat through the castle's rear exit. Merlin slowly made his way through the Keep to seek out Arthur. Melin found Guinevere and Morgana Le fay; Arthur's, half-sister, huddled together in an aunty room.

"My ladies, I am your servant. I am here to help. Mordred has left the castle and no longer holds sway over this place." Guinevere replied.

"Merlin, this can not be you. Much time has passed since we last spoke, yet you have not aged a day."

"I am Morgana Le fay; no doubt you have heard my name in mention. You must be the famous Merlin I've heard so much of. Your magic has not been overstated; you truly do command the powers of nature. Your visit has been long overdue and most welcomed at this time. We've been little more than prisoners in this place for this last year or more. Her Majesty has not been well of late, and I have tended to her needs in these difficult times. Mordred has ruled over the kingdom in the absence of the king. He was supported by the Lady of the Lake: The King's once trusted friend and adviser. It was she who suggested Mordred should be made steward of the kingdom in Arthur's absence. This deception all started with Sir Lancelot's unsolicited advances to the Queen. A cleverly devised plot to split the court with roomers and subversive activity. After Sir Lancelot was forced to leave, he stirred up trouble on the continent, compelling King Arthur to begin his campaign there. In Arthur's absence, they then schemed together to pillage the land through heavy taxation. She also conspired with Mordred sending false reports to King Arthur that all was well. By supplying him with enough funds to extend his campaign, they were able to keep King Arthur away for so much longer than he had intended. Although it cannot be proven, we suspect they were secretly giving Lancelot financial support also: Lancelot, in turn, aided the Saxons to prolong the conflict and further his own ambitions."

"I know how close you were to The Lady of the Lake Merlin, but all that Lady Morgana has said is true."

"His plan was to attack the King and his battle-weary knights as they entered the castle. He had planned to kill Arthur then claim the throne as his birthright. King Arthur has been kept abroad fighting Saxons far too long at the kingdom's expense. Such is the consequence of this war under the stewardship of these two scheming villains."

"I Have been with Ruth, the true Lady of the Lake, all this time and since I last departed this place. I can assure you that lookalike imposter Nimue of Avalon was the woman I saw on your Wedding day, Queen Guinevere. She is not The Lady of the Lake. Lady Ruth is that person, do you now remember?"

"Yes, now you have brought that to mind. I do recall the resemblance of the two young women. My health and memory are not what they were. Over the years, memory does favour such a deceptive role and the King's acceptance of her. To him, she only said she was The Lady of the Lake and never uttered the name Ruth or Nimue. Merlin, it is good you are here. We must make ready for the arrival of the King: A welcome he truly deserves. Will you oversee the defence of Camalot until King Arthur's arrival?"

"I am always at your service, Your Majesty. I will take my leave and go inform the captain of the guard of your intentions." He gave a grin before saying. "There are also some repairs required concerning the main road before King Arthur's arrival."

Within the next few days, Merlin was able to bring some form of order and appearance to what had rapidly become a castle in disarray.

The walls flanking the front gates had been painted with limewash, and general maintenance now given priority was well underway. Camalot was starting to look like the welcoming place it was intended to be. With lookouts situated in strategic areas, and guards patrolling their positions once more with pride, all was ready for the King's triumphant return. There was now little for Merlin to do but wait. He used this time to stratify the King's best next move against Mordred. A conflict Merlin saw as inevitable. The plan, he was convinced to be the best one, was to wait. These laps in time he hoped would fool Mordred into a false sense of security. This respite would also give Arthur's battle-wiry army time to recuperate. Arthur could then choose the time and place for this inevitable showdown with a reinvigorated army full of confidence. A significant obstacle to overcome in his plan was: How he would restrain an angry King. To quail the King's emotions so cooler heads can prevail; must be his first task. He saw it as a foolhardy move to charge headlong into Mordred's stronghold unprepared and without a battle plan. Yes, this must be the point he must emphasize to Arthur. Lady Morgana entered the main hall and sat next to Merlin to speak with him at the round table.

"Soon after the King has taken command of the castle, I will request to take my leave from this place. I will require an escort of trusted men. I wish to take back my place as the true Lady of Avalon. I intend to overthrow this imposter Nimue. The Isle of Avalon is mine by right. When I control Avalon's Vale, it will again serve as a stronghold for his Majesty. I can help him command his southwest domain from this stronghold. It would not be wise to leave Queen Guinevere alone in her condition. If King Arthur intends to mount his campaign against Mordred soon after his arrival, her needs must be considered. Perhaps at that point, she should visit the convent at Amesbury. There she could be tended to by nuns who are skilled in the art of clinical care."

"That is a valid point, Lady Morgana. I will support you in any way

I can. Perhaps the King would allow me to be part of that escort you require." At this point, she placed her hand on his and looked lovingly into his eyes. This move did not come as a complete surprise to him as he had noticed her unsolicited attention towards him of late. For her, it was an attempt to escalate a relationship that had never been encouraged by Merlin. The coy glances and the subtle flick of her head to display her flowing locks had not gone unnoticed. Trivial excuses were also used to garner any opportunity that could be construed necessary enough to require his company. This was her way of showing her attraction towards him. Her ultimate wish was to take their relationship to a new level.

How was Merlin to discourage this attention without seeming discourteous? His heart totally belonged to Ruth. Although Morgana was a good caring woman and a woman any man would be proud to walk beside: His true love was Ruth. It was a dilemma.

"My lady, when you look into my eyes in such a way, it reminds me of the way my Lady Ruth looks at me on such occasions. In those moments, her looks can pierce my very soul, then hold it and mould it as if it were clay in her hands. She can then command me to do whatsoever she wills. For she knows I will always be her passionate, loving servant. Some day there will be a man whose feelings for you will be so strong he will melt like butter in your hands. Only then will you know you have found your one true love, but I am not he." He then placed his other hand over hers and caressed it gently. He felt the hurt mixed with the slight embarrassment she must be now experiencing. For him, he saw no other way to convey his own feelings of friendship for her and nothing more. "Rest assured, Lady Morgana, there will always be a small place for you in my heart also, but it is a heart already taken."

"I think I understand, and on reflection, would not have respected you had you forsaken your true love so easily." She slowly pulled her hand away and, in an attempt to alter the mood reverted to their original conversation.

As for your offer to ride at my side, I'm sure a show of force would no longer be necessary to unseat this usurper Nimue."

There was a call from the battlements (The King is on his way and will be here soon.)

"We must make ourselves ready to greet the King, my Lady. There is much to be conveyed to him, and I suggest this should be done with the greatest diplomacy. He must be persuaded to view all the circumstances with a level head to fully understand the ramifications of what has happened and what must happen. Only then can we move forward with confidence to enact the plans I have set out for him to prevail over Mordred."

Arthur arrived with all the pomp and ceremony of a conquering hero. Although it was a wiry-looking army that entered the castle: They were still able to maintain that air of dignity required of them.

Arthur was ushered to the great hall for a debriefing that he would not be pleased to hear. However, Merlin took it upon himself to be the bearer of the disturbing news knowing the King's anger would be hard to contain. When Arthur's rage had settled down somewhat, Merlin managed to convince him that cooler heads must prevail. These new goals must succeed. And so careful planning would need to be adhered to. He then continued to explain the strategy he had envisioned to win the day. How to draw Mordred from his stronghold, divide his force, then engage the spilt divisions individually. This way, Arthur's army would be able to overwhelm Mordred's depleted main army by sheer numbers. It was quite an elaborate plan to draw Mordred out and split his forces, so Merlin requested that he alone should lead their own decoy company of men. There was also another detail to be considered. The Queen's heath should be prioritized tended to immediately. He then explained in full detail his battle plan.

"We must split his force by deception. This will work well in our favour. First, your Majesty, I would beg your leave to act as escort to the Queen. This would be only for the first part of her journey. We will then assign her a small escort to take her the remainder of the way to Amesbury. Lady Morgana and I will then continue on at great speed; to fulfill her quest to regain Avalon. My plan is when I leave Camalot with the Queen and Lady Morgana's escort, we take most of your army and let it be known of our intentions to take Avalon by force. Then under cover of night, the main part of that force would return to Comealot, making it again your main command. I'm sure Mordred has spies still amongst us. They will surely report this major split of your forces as soon as we leave. I anticipate him sending a small, fast force across the Chanel and down the coast in ships to sure up defences on the Isle of Avalon. That way, this force can bypass Camalot's defences completely without being challenged. He will then be lured out from his stronghold to attack what he perceives as an unsuspecting main force from the rear, bypassing an undermanned Comealot. This will then give you the opportunity after he has passed you by to follow him. My small force will have taken care of his sea assault and wait for him at Camlann hill fort before he arrives. We should be able to hold him off and await your army's arrival to crush him between us. This is my plan, my King."

"What of your small force Merlin? How will you fare against a reinforced Avalon?"

"There are catapults at Camlann hill fort. We will move them by raft across the marsh flats to engage the ships on their approach to The Isle of Avalon. For this, we must make great haste in the execution of our quest. There will be no margin for error."

"It sounds like a sound plan. Your absence will be sorely missed, but the needs of the state must prevail. I wish you a safe journey, and may good fortune be with you. Until we meet at Camlann Merlin." Arthur stood face to face to embrace Merlin before Merlin left to prepare for his new mission. "God speed, my friend."

CHAPTER 16

Ruth arrived back at the archeological site she'd departed from with Peter only seconds before in this Now. Those thunderous noises she'd heard on departure, she quickly identified. 'They're definitely explosions. Yes, those are explosions; and neither were those flashes I'd glimpsed lighting.' There was also the distinctive sound of gunfire erupting from down the mountain. I came from the general direction of the base camp. Her anxiety level was beginning to rise. These were her colleagues and friends that were in this danger zone. She ran from the gate down the dirt road towards base camp. As she ran, her strides became longer, and the roadway looked nothing more than a narrow path. It was not until she'd reached base camp did the realization of her actual size become apparent. Even in Petra, she had not grown this large. A man approached her with a gun and started to fire. It all looked so slow. He looked at her. The fear in his eyes reflected every emotion and vibration his body was creating. It was being emitted to her like some personalized radio signal. She could see through this outer veneer of his body into his very soul. His fears, his aspirations and intentions; she saw everything. The stream of bullets from his gun was brushed aside as if they were no more than water jets from a hose. He dropped the gun and stood in silence, awaiting his punishment.

Justice was swift. With the brush of her hand, he'd been pushed aside. He then fell over the edge of the roadway. She gave no concern. Her only thought was to reach base camp. Upon arrival, it was not the sight she'd hoped to see. Several of her friends lay dead beside bullet-riddled tents. There were blackened potholes in the ground, marking the spots of the explosions she had heard. They had obviously put up some kind of resistance against this unprovoked attack. Where was the motivation to provoke such violence? Her friends had no political or religious agendas to warrant such barbaric treatment.

Her next thoughts were, 'where was the rest of the team. Were they still alive and in hiding? Perhaps they had been taken hostage, or even worse, they too were dead?' She would waste no time leaving this place to get answers to these questions. It then occurred to her there was probably a companion to the terrorist she had dispatched so unceremoniously. She had a new agenda, fine this other piece of crap and get whatever information she could from him. Her anger by now had got the better of her. Her rage was way beyond control, but she did not care. As she scanned the surrounding area, she had the distinct feeling she was being watched. He could not hide from her. She could sense his fear. His every thought his emotions were acting like homing beacons, enabling her to easily detect his exact location. As she approached his hiding place, he stood up. He then pointed a grenade launcher at her and fired. Catching the missile in mid-flight, she turned it on its axis and lunched it straight back at him. "Where are the people that were here? What's been done with them? Are they still alive and safe?"

"Yes, yes, they've been taken for ransom and moved by truck to our headquarters."

"Where is that? I need to know now."

"Down the mountain and seven miles due north. But who are you?

What are you, a goddess?"

"I am Petra, the GateKeeper. Now answer my questions."

"Yes, your highness. It was not my decision. I begged my compadres not to do this terrible thing, but I am but a lowly soldier. Please, I was only obeying orders; please spare me. I implore you." This pleading was a distraction. Stashed in the back of his belt was a handgun. 'Yes, these were empty words flowing from his mouth. He'd anticipated such an event as this taking place and had not been truthful in what he had said. There was no remorse for his own actions. The rhetoric flowing from his mouth was no more than empty words intended to mask his true intentions.' Ruth saw through this charade. It was not hard for her to see his true intentions, having the ability to look deep into his soul.

"You made your choice when you took up arms. Whoever lives by the sword dies by the sword. Make your choice now." He quickly pointed his weapon and fired, hoping to catch her off guard. Anticipating his action, she had already sent back his own projectile to stop only feet from the end of his automatic's gun barrel. This brief instant should have given him time to evaluate his decision, but his reaction was clouded by hatred rather than common sense. The end result, the bullet from his own weapon, hit the projectile head-on. It was not a pretty sight. This gave Ruth misgivings for her own actions, but it was by his own hand he'd met this gruesome but quick demise.

Exerting the dominant role of A Gatekeeper more comfortably, Ruth used all the judgement and authority at her command to make this decision. These lost souls were going to purgatory and definitely not heaven. It took but a blink of an eye in this Now to greet their souls at the gate. She talked of future redemption. It was explained where they were going and how bad choices in the lives they had just departed had determined where they were about to be sent. She then spoke of why both men should take this time in purgatory to contemplate their choices in life.

Specific choices determine where the paths we tread will lead. Meditation would provide an understanding of how they could avoid similar pitfalls in a future existence. You both should be fully aware of why you are being sent to this place you are about to enter. She also went on to say: When fully accepting and understanding the responsibility for life's decisions, perhaps then and only then would reincarnation be granted. This would be a way to revisit the trials and tribulations life throws at an individual. Hopefully, this experience, through some ingrained knowledge, would enhance a future existence. Perhaps it will take you many journeys on life's rocky road before you understand the goals that you will set yourselves. Only you, yourselves, can genuinely evaluate your motives accurately. Who could give a more accurate analysis of your actions than you? Think of reincarnation as writing lines on a blackboard. Perhaps it will take one hundred times to fully understand the meaning of your existence. This being said, she dispatched these two lost souls before returning to the Now she had just left.

Her first priority was to dig some shallow resting places for her friends. After laying their bodies to rest, she filled the graves before covering them with stones. Although there was a sense of urgency for the tasks that lay ahead of her, she still found time for a minute of silence and sadness for her fallen companions.

One of her team's vehicles looked fully operational. Probably left as transportation for the two recently dispatched terrorists, the cleanup crew. This could work well for Ruth as initially, the terrorists might mistake her for one of their comrades. She jumped in and started the engine. Tucking her hair up under a hat she'd donned that had been lying on the front seat would help with this deception. Feeling there was no time to lose, she drove much faster than any sane person would have. Using her enhanced ability, this all seemed so easy. If the location she had been told was correct, she should now be within less than a mile of her destination.

As she slowed down, not wishing to drive straight into the camp, she had time to contemplate how she could have changed this whole scenario, or still could. After leaving with Peter, she could have returned before her departure and intervened in those recent events before they had taken place. She could also leave this place and return at any given time, being more informed. Then she thought of what Peter had told her about how altering the past affected the future. In his words (To change one word could change the sentence; by adjusting a sentence, you've changed the chapter and perhaps the whole book.) 'Yes, things must unfold as they will in this, Now, as I am a part of these events. For me, everything I do must not be affected by any previous knowledge. If I had lived through past events and then gone back to change them as I saw fit, the lives I might be affecting would be unfathomable. I now see why Peter always let me shape events rather than him. It was because he did have previous knowledge of those events.'

Philosophizing complete, her thoughts then turned to the matters at hand. Deciding to reconnoitre on foot first, she pulled the truck over to the side of the road. Making her way to where she believed the camp was, she kept close to the edge of the road. This was to help avoid detection. A clearing up ahead contained several small huts, Ruth's thoughts, where this must be the place. 'I'll hide in the bush where I can observe what's happening. This will help in assessing the situation.' There were several men with automatic weapons walking around the camp. 'Too much of a surprise for these terrorists could result in indiscriminate gunfire. This could do more harm than good, resulting in more of her friends being hurt or killed. No, this would not do. Surprise still seemed the best option. That hut over there is heavily guarded. This must be where my friends are being held captive. This could work well for me. I'll drive into camp, and before they can identify me, I'll park the truck in front of the hut. Hopefully, I could also take the guard in front of the hut with the truck by this maneuver. It would also give cover to the hut should gunfire erupted.' There was another upside to this plan; her friends inside the hut would not see any supper human acts that would undoubtedly take place. It would not be easy to keep such a secrete from the world if viewed by such reliable witnesses as the archeological team she'd worked with.

Using stealth, she made her way back to the truck. Taking a deep breath, she set her plan into motion. Driving into camp, she'd hit the guard and took him out before a shot had been fired. Quickly leaving the truck, her intention was to draw fire away from the hut. The plan up to this point was working well. A sweeping motion from her hand diverted bullets like fallen leaves from a tree blown by the wind. Into the air, projectiles rose; only to drop back from where they had come from. They were like rain from the sky falling. It was time to demonstrate a little more of her power. Ruth was confident she had absolute control of all her abilities. She grew in size to as large as she possibly could. This supernatural display was all that was needed to convince any terrorist with any fight left in him to beat a hasty retreat. Ruth then seized this opportunity to free her friends before the terrorists regained their courage and mounted a counter-attack. Reverting back to her original size, she threw the bolt on the hut door and rescued her friends. As they emerged into the fading daylight, it still took a short time for their eyes to adjust from the darkness of the hut that had been their resent prison.

"We must move quickly. Pick up any weapons you see lying around, then fined some transportation. I'll drive our truck. Any vehicles we can't take, destroy by any means possible, let's move it." Team leader Joe Farmer jumped into the truck with Ruth. She then drove around the camp at speed, acting as cover for the rest of the team. Joe did his part by firing off a few rounds from a weapon he'd acquired. This gave the team more leeway to accomplish the tasks Ruth had asked them to do. When the last person had boarded a vehicle, she bellowed out, "Let's move out, people." This order was given with a tone of earnest authority. This display of leadership and Ruth's command ability got a surprised stare from Joe.

As they drove down the road, Joe again looked at Ruth, almost in disbelief. "Where did that shy young lady that I once knew go, and when did she become an army commander."

"You and the team should make for the nearest town. I won't be going with you. My destiny takes a different path, or I should say, has already taken that path. Much has happened since I last saw you."

"Ruth, we were only attacked and taken prisoner just hours ago. What could have possibly happened in such a short space of time to have changed your life so dramatically."

"If I told you, you would not believe me."

"Please try me. I've seen some strange things in my lifetime."

"O.K. Here goes, take a deep breath and prepare to hear the unbelievable. I went to Athens, met Pericles, visited Stonehenge, schooled a young King Arthur, fell in love with Merlin, the magician, saw Petra and put down a rebellion there."

"Oh, and that's it, all in about an hour, I'm guessing. That must be some travel agent you booked with."

"There, I told you you wouldn't believe me. Oh, I didn't tell you about the trip to the future I took. That was exciting and most informative. Wait for it; this will really blow your mind; apparently, I'm a descendent of a Greek goddess. Well, not too distant a descendent apparently, I'm a granddaughter." She felt some sort of relief and pleasure at unloading this information on a disbelieving Joe.

"Ruth, what have you been smoking. You've never been delusional or taken to fantasizing. Where are all these tall tales coming from?" The front tire blew out with a loud bang at that exact moment. This sent the truck scraping sidelong against the cliff face beside them before she regained control. The impact weakened the lower face causing some subsidence there. This, in turn, dislodged some heave rocks that were embedded in the sandstone cliff face above. A large boulder from behind this disturbance slid free, rolling at first, then bouncing downwards. It Hit another rock, which diverted its course. It was then sent careering towards the truck's cab. "Ruth, jump for your life." Joe opened his door and was ready to jump. He again looked at Ruth. "Jump, for goodness sake, jump."

"It's alright. Everything is under control. Close your door."

With a pushing motion of her hand, the rock floated like a cloud before elevating itself into the air. It then glided silently overhead to drop harmlessly down into the valley below. She then pushed the truck safely away from the cliff face using the same hand motion. Sweeping all remaining debris from the road with a swish of her hand, she jumped out to tend to their flat.

"Get the spare and the wheel wrench Joe." He was about to mention the jack when he saw Ruth elevate the front of the vehicle. He froze in astonishment. "Joe, the wheel," she shouted loudly and with authority. Joe shook his head in disbelief before continuing his task of getting the wheel from the back of the truck. She then levitated a large rock lying beside the road and manoeuvred it under the vehicle to support its weight well, replacing the damaged wheel. Once in place, she lowered the truck back down. The rest of the team had arrived at the accident and were quick to help replace the wheel. Ruth again gave the orders. "Back to your vehicles, people, let's go."

"Your truck still has that rock wedged under it." One of the team replied.

"Don't worry, I think I can just back the truck off it, no problem" As she started the truck, Joe jumped in, well the rest of the crew ran back to their respective vehicles. With a downward pushing motion of her hand, the front rose enough to clear the rock as they backed away. All this happened unseen by a team intent on returning to their vehicles well facing the opposite direction.

Driving on down the road, Joe looked at Ruth in amazement. "I thought you were off your head, but after what I've just witnessed, I don't know what to think. What happened to you that allowed you to do these other wonderful things you've told me you've done. How did you change into this supper being? If you must leave, there's so little time for you to tell me more so, please continue with your story."

"I'll be as brief as possible. There's a portal on the mountain, and I was taken through it by my father. He guards the gates, for there are many. My D.N.A. and the use of a special code allow me to travel through time and space to whichever place or time I wish to visit. Needless to say, my preference was to visit archeological sights and historical events. On one such trip, I was given a title by King Arthur himself. When he was a prince, I saved him from drowning. He nor Guinevere could swim, so I insisted on teaching them both in that same lake that so nearly took his life. He named me (The lady of the Lake). No doubt you've heard that name mentioned." She gave a chuckle. "Well, now you can put a face to it. I will not age, so I will be as you see me today when you see me many years in the future. Perhaps I can tell you then where Excalibur can be found. As legend has it, it is I who took it for safekeeping. When you drop me off, please don't mention a word of what I've told you to anyone."

"Why would I do that. I wouldn't want to be labelled insane or delusional. A statement of that nature would servilely jeopardize my career without supportive evidence. And I'm sure there are no other eyewitnesses to any of the events that have taken place, are there?"

"No, I'm always cautious about what events have been witnessed and by whom. It is important to maintain the correct linear flow of history."

"So, tell me more about your father. Why does he guard these gates, and for what purpose? If you have time, I'd be very interested to know all about it."

"The portals or gates can only be entered by your soul or ghost. It turns you into an opalescent spectral of light when you are about to enter. You may then enter the gateway to heaven, and yes, Peter, who meets you at that gate, is my father. I am a gatekeeper in training, so to speak."

"Have you greeted any souls at the gate yourself, Ruth?"

"I have, and I'm amazed at the wisdom I've seemed to have acquired. It's wisdom far beyond my life span of experience. I can look into a person's inner being and help them evaluate their lives. It's so uncanny, but I feel I am only here to help, and that makes it all feel good. I hope I won't meet you in my role as gatekeeper for a very long time, Joe. When your time does come, I will be there for you; rest assured. Well, this is my stop, Joe, so take the wheel and may good luck follow you." With that said, she jumped from the truck and waved goodbye to the team. There was a tear in her eye. Ruth knew she was also saying goodbye to this life she had loved. It was a long walk back to the gate, and darkness had closed in on her before her arrival. Taking one long last look around, she then slipped through the portal.

CHAPTER 17

The road to Amesbury was well travelled, but it was in poor condition through lack of maintenance as with most other routes. It took more time than Merlin had initially estimated to complete the first leg of this journey. When they were safely beyond any perceived danger, the Queen and her escort were dispatched and continued to their particular destination. It was then a race against time to make the ancient Camlann Hillfort in the Vale of Avalon. Would this place welcome them or show resistance? Only time would tell?

The towering slopes of Camlann Hill allowed the fortifications built on top to dominate the flats below it. Camlann Hill resembled a large oval-shaped pie dish turned upside down onto the Vale of Avalon's flat surface below. It presented a formidable site to any would-be aggressor.

It was decided to approach in a single file with standers flying. Showing the King's collars would identify who they were. If they were to come under fire, only the vanguard would face the full brunt of an attack.

It was an unarmed delegation of the populace that greeted them. These were people that had been overtaxed under the tyranny of Nimue. Chants of "The King Has Returned. The King Has Returned, Long live the King. Long live the King." This was a warmer welcome than any of this King's army could have hoped for.

When Merlin explained his need for the catapults, men knowledgeable in their use were quick to volunteer their services to the cause. Braking them down into transportable pieces was an easy task for experienced operators of these weapons of war.

Their trek across the flats went well, and when the salt marshes surrounding the Isle of Avalon were reached, rafts were built. After reassembling the catapults on the sturdy platforms. All that was left for them to do was wait for high tide. The tides of this channel being amongst the highest rise and fall in the known world would work well from Merlin's plan. It made it easy to position their artillery in a commanding position when this mash land became a shallow sea. Once in place, the task of camouflaging began. Soon all that was visible to the naked eye was what looked to be outcroppings of vegetation.

Early next morning, they staged their assault on the Island at low tide. Merlin was surprised to find the stronghold undermanned. It was quickly overrun after some bitter fighting. Morgana was now reinstated in her fortress; it was time to interrogate prisoners.

It quickly became apparent Nimue had fled to the southeast coast directly after her encounter with Merlin at Camalot. This was disturbing. Was she looking for reinforcements from Arthur's enemies on the continent or just fleeing Morgana's wrath?

A courier was immediately sent to inform Arthur of what could be perceived as a new threat. Even a small force from the east could unhinge Merlin's well-conceived plan. All that could be hoped for at this point in the operation would be for Arthur to overwhelm Mordred's army with a swift victory. Hopefully, his surprise attack from the rear would make this possible. This would then alleviate any new threat before it could materialize. His small band had no choice but to continue with their allotted job. The following morning ships were sighted in the channel. They would have to wait for high tide to move in close enough to disembark their troops. This gave ample time to prepare for the warm welcome that had been so carefully planned.

Patiently they waited until the ships were close and committed before unleashing the power of the catapults. The attack was devastating. Massive rocks rained from the sky, smashing the fleet to pieces. Troops clad in armour had little chance of survival, even in these shallow waters. A bone-chilling cold quickly sapped the energy from struggling drowning men. There was no time to savour this swift victory. Time was at the essence to effectively assist in the primary battle that would undoubtedly start soon.

As the small force reached the flats surrounding Camlann Hill, they could see Mordred's army approaching southwards in the distance. It was essential this foot race to Camlann Hill must be won. Arriving at the hill first did not prove to be a problem. However, the climb did depleted much of their energy. It was a band of weary men that were now preparing to face and repel this much larger force. Without catapults to disrupt a frontal assault that would undoubtedly be using a shield wall could prove difficult. Some means to keep the attacking force at bay for a sustained amount of time must be found; otherwise, the consequences could prove catastrophic. Merlin turned to his catapult crews for help.

"Is there any heavy weaponry left in the fort?" The catapult captain answered.

"We have two old Roman Vitruvius ballista's stored in a shed over there." he pointed in the direction of a dilapidated old building. "They may still be serviceable. These ancient small rock-throwing heavy crossbows have not seen the light of day in many a year. With some careful handling, we may be able to coax a few good shots out of them. Their two-pound projectiles are more than capable of smashing through a shield wall." They were quickly cleaned up, serviced and towed up to the top of the fort's defences.

"There's little time to lose. We must make this happen." He then turned to the other fort dwellers. "Have you a grain mill here." Yes, was the reply. "Fetch the wheel. We will mount a massive long shaft through it and then fit wheels at each end of that shaft. We must then place it outside the fort, ready to roll down the hill into an unsuspecting advancing army. With their shield wall up, it will be difficult for them to perceive what is happening before it's too late.

It took ten men to lift the heavy wheel from its mountings and roll it outside the gate. Once there, the shaft was fitted and end wheels mounted. One of the men suggested that nails could be hammered into the beam to make it more lethal as a finishing touch. It was then camouflaged with grass to hide the surprise they hoped to bring to the advancing army on their initial assault. They had done all they could possibly do. It was time to wait.

From the high advantage point of the fort walls, a lookout spotted Arthur's army approaching. Their trap was about to be sprung. Mordred's focus on a quick victory by taking the fort by storm blinded his view of the approaching army at his rear. He was also relying on his army from the west. He had no way of knowing it no longer existed. With confidence, he mounted his assault. The shield wall advanced as expected, and behind it, shielded from arrows, was a battering ram. The hill's steep slopes proved to be a more laborious task than was expected. It was challenging to tow such a substantial piece of equipment up this rise. The result being the shield wall was moving too fast to give adequate cover to a lumbering battering ram crew. Archers from the fort were then able to take advantage of this breakdown in coordination. Mordred's losses were heavy under a steady rain of arrows as the shield wall moved forward. Time to unleash the power of the Ballista. They concentrated on the flanks, and when their work was done, the mill wheel was rolled at their centre. This carefully conceived plan had worked beyond expectations. Archers were able to concentrate their fire at vulnerable infantry. They were left unprotected after the defeat of a once impregnable to arrows, shield wall. The carnage left strewn on the hill was stomach-churning even for battle-hardened mature fighting men. This first assault had been successfully repelled. Mordred's assault force retreated and regrouped at the bottom of the hill with his main army. They remained safely out of range of any weaponry the fort possessed. He intended his next assault to be planned much differently. This first attempt by Mordred had been nothing more than a test of the fort's defences. His lean dark figure sitting tall in the saddle would look ominous to anyone facing this army. However, the defenders were aware of the battle plan envisioned by Merlin.

Mordred summoned his captains to convey his next strategy. "This is obviously just a small contingent of Arthur's main force we're dealing with. If our next attack is from all sides, there is no possible way these defenders can protect such a large circumference. Once one of my many arms has breached the walls, we will quickly overrun the fort. This time we will use grappling irons to scale the walls. Archers will provide cover fire.

His main force must still be held at bay by my troops on the Island of Avalon. Once we have taken the fort, we will be able crush Arthur from the rear. He will be trapped with his back to the sea and bogged down in the marshes with nowhere to run. You know what I require from each and every one of you. Should anyone fail in their duty, they can wish for a quick death, but it will not be granted. Go forth and fulfil your assignments." His army then spilt into coulombs to surround the fort. It was not until they were fully deployed did Mordred realize Arthur's army was upon him.

Immediately he saw the disaster that was about to befall him. Before he could regroup his men, Arthur had attacked the coulombs with the full strength of his army. These strung-out lines were unable to withstand the onslaught that was taking place. Surrounded on each side by the concentration of overwhelming numbers, Mordred's army was being taken apart piecemeal. Arthur's men moved along Mordred's coulombs, mowing men down like a sickle through the grass.

When all looked lost for Mordred, Nimue was sighted to the east. She had assembled a ragtag band of Saxon mercenaries from across the channel. This distraction and balance in numbers could give all the time required for Mordred to fall back and regroup. Arthur was now obliged to split his main force to confront this new threat. As the tide of battle turned, a regrouped army, spurred on by an enraged Mordred, made a counterattack. This time Mordred had the advantage of numbers over Arthur's split forces. The battle raged on with bitter hand-to-hand fighting combining two intertwining armies into one bloody death dance.

Merlin tried to create a black hole close to Nimue's division, but he found his power could not extend that far. He then ordered his small force to follow him and join the fray. Leaving the fort to confront Nimue's army, Merlin spearheaded this reinforced strike force sent by Arthur. By the time he was close enough to open a black hole, Arthur's men were too close to Nimue's division for him to safely accomplish this. With the help of the fort's extra manpower, they could now push this new threat from the east to the south and then westward.

A welcome sight appeared to the west in the shape of Morgana's small force. Nimue was now trapped between two of Arthur's forces. When this battle was all but over, Merlin left Morgana to reap her revenge. He left this battle to join Arthur, who was under stress in his struggle by fragmenting his own army forced to fight on so many fronts.

Testosterone-fuelled rage took a grip on Arthur as he saw Mordred clearly for the first time in this battle. He was in the back ranks of his army, ridding too and fro spurring on his men. Arthur pointed Excalibur at his foe and charged. His brave knights followed blindly into the midst of Mordred's main force. A foolhardy move, but heroic deeds are often preceded by foolishness. Mordred's ranks split as Arthur's sudden attack broke through his opposition like an axe striking through kindling. Arthur soon reached his quarry. Some heavy blows from Excalibur unseated Mordred from his mount. Arthur savoured the final pointed thrust that ended any hope of Mordred's victory.

In a last attempt to save their commander, a simultaneous barrage of arrows rained on Arthur's elite force that had followed him so bravely. Merlin was too late to stop this rain of arrows from decimating the group of heroes, but his glowing sword soon cleared enough breathing space for the wounded to be rescued by Arthur's army. If Merlin created a black hole so close, it would be as dangerous to friends as their foes. He then took command to quickly finish a battle that had annihilated the cream of the kingdoms fighting men. Scouring the battlefield close by, it was strewn with dead and wounded. He found Arthur amongst the fallen. Arthur was in critical condition. Arrows from several bows had done their work to bring down this mighty worrier King. Now, he summoned a soldier to take an urgent message to Morgana to come quickly at Arthur's side. There were still some isolated skirmishes taking place. Sealing the fate of the remaining remnants of Mordred's army so soon accomplished. Distracted by Arthur's plight, Merlin did not see the arrow fired from a bowman lying close by and thought dead. It struck Merlin in his side: This was possibly a mortal wound. He slumped to the ground beside his King. Sir Bedivere, whose sword had been broken in battle, took up Excalibur and dispatched this fallen archer before he could do more damage.

Morgana arrived to take control as Bedivere stood guard over his King and Merlin; well, their wounds were simultaneously tended to. Arthur beckoned Bedivere to come close. "Take Excalibur and cast it into the lake where the Lady of the Lake once saved my life."

"Your Majesty, if that is your will, so be it." He started to walk away but then looked at the sword and turned back. "I find this quest you have tasked me with almost impossible to perform, your Majesty."

"It is my will. Please go now, my brave knight." Again Bedivere tried to walk away but paused. "It has been decided by fate; this should happen, don't ask me how I know this. I just know." He bowed to his King.

"Your Majesty, I will carry out your wish to the letter." This time he left to fulfil the task he had pledged to complete.

Morgana spoke to the two wounded she was tending. "I will have you both taken to Amesbury. Guinevere will be waiting there for you both."

Merlin's eyes opened, and he looked to Morgana to assist him with his request. "Please have me taken to the gorge, it's a special place for me, and I feel compelled to go there."

"If that is your wish, Master Merlin, so be it. I will make it so." As Merlin and Arthur bid their last farewells to each other, arrangements were made for both journeys.

Merlin's trip was not an easy one. With every bump in the road came the risk of more blood loss. He knew he had to remain conscious to guide his litter to the hidden portal in the gorge. He knew he had to go there, but he was unsure for what purpose. On arrival at the Cheddar Gorge, his litter captain also questioned why they had brought him to this place. As they spoke, Ruth appeared from the cleft in the rock. She was shocked to see Merlin's condition but immediately knew the remedy. She had sensed the need to visit the portal at this time.

"This way, quickly." Ushering them into the narrow cleft, she placed Merlin's hand on the keyed tablet and helped him push in the sequence of numbers unique to him. She then thrust his body through the portal.

"What have you done, my lady. You have made him a prisoner of the rock." She smiled.

"Have no fear he will be fit to fight another day soon enough. Please tell me, what was the catastrophe that brought you to this place?"

"There has been a great battle between many armies. King Arthur's followers took the day but at a high cost. Many lives were lost, especially among the ranks of his Knights in their last decisive charge that won the battle. The King himself, mortally wounded, has been taken to Amesbury, where there are nuns skilled in the art of healing.

Can we be of service to you in any way, My Lady?"

"Yes, I need a horse. I fear there's little time to waste. There's one more task I must complete before I leave to join Merlin. Now I feel there's an appointment I must attend. It concerns a sword, I believe. So I will bid you all farewell and you to good captain." Saying those words, she took a horse from him and headed south.

There was only one lake she felt Arthur would return Excalibur to. It was the one where she had saved his life on that warm summer day so many years before, in Arthur's time. Bedivere was already standing on the bank at the lake's far side when Ruth arrived. Jumping from the horse, she ran to the lake. Slipping on the silt at the edge of the water, she ungraciously slid into the bulrushes that were abundant in this bank. All of this commotion went unnoticed by Bedivere, who was still fighting his own emotions to discard such an iconic sword. A symbolic weapon that once united a kingdom. It would mean the end of Comealot and the Knights of the round table for him. On the last day, at this last minute, was a precise moment that would end an era. Ruth was now in her own miner turmoil and caught up in the moment she swam to open water before surfacing.

As she came up for air Excalibur, fell from the sky towards her. She slowed its descent considerably with the use of her power. Putting a hand skyward, she quickly grasped it by the handle. She then elevated herself out of the water. Bedivere waved to her.

His recollection of The Lady of the Lake had been imprinted in his mind. As a young boy, he was always beguiled by her beauty.

Ruth's image had been embroidered into his memory from her portrait, hanging in that place of honour at Camealot. That image had initiated a puppy love relationship he had always nurtured. The first stirrings of sexual emotions in that young boy so long ago was a memory that had forever stayed with him. That image was now indelibly impressed in his mind and always would be as only the unobtainable dream can be.

Once Ruth had made it back to shore, she decided to take Excalibur back to Cheddar Gorge. It was the place it was first drawn from the stone by fire. She pondered where to place it for safekeeping as she travelled.

'Perhaps the cave or under its stone of origin. Yes, that would be the perfect place.' Her mind now set, she made for the spot where Merlin had first shown her the effigy trapped in stone. She remembered that long summer evening in that, Now, that seemed so long ago for her.

She used the sword to dig a hole deep enough to hold it safe for future generations to behold. Wrapping it in the horse blanket, she carefully placed it, pointing downwards into the hole. All this was meticulously done, so it could be rediscovery at a later date. This was done to shed light on the true legend of King Arthur. When this task had been accomplished, all that was left to do was tell Joe Farmer of its whereabouts. This was her last thought before revisiting the portal.

CHAPTER 18

Stepping out the same portal but into a different era than the one she just left became apparent because of her dress. She'd only stepped but a few feet when Merlin followed her through. He was now in perfect health. There was no arrow wound and no blood loss. He checked himself out thoroughly then looked at Ruth with a sense of amazement. "How can this be? I was dying."

"Yes, a little thing I neglected to tell you was when you go through the gate, it restores your body to the original state of your very first entry. That's why we'll never age. And that's also the reason I pushed you through so quickly."

"I see, although it does not surprise me, for you have never aged since the first day we met. As you say, there is so much to learn. Perhaps you could explain how, when I entered the portal first, I exited here after you instead of before."

"Time does not exist as you know it, another strange fact for you to get used to. Don't worry, I'll be your teacher, as always." She gave him a dig with her elbow and laughed.

"Your dress, these clothes, they are all strange to me. Comfortable but strange."

"This is the twenty-first century, Merlin. I have a coin in my pocket dated twenty twelve, and it doesn't look new, so we're in an era later than that date. The battle you just fought at Camlann may feel like yesterday to you, but in this, Now, it was perhaps sixteen hundred years ago or so." This made him feel uneasy, and he seemed a little bewildered. "Come, we must find transportation to Bristol."

"Can we not visit Camalot."

"It's not known as Camalot in this Now. And in this, Now, it's been lost to time. Today Bristol stands in its place, but only you and I would know that. You see, another great castle was built over its foundations, so probably that's the reason it's never been discovered."

"Then we should visit this new castle. We can tell of its glorious past."

"Well, that castle no longer stands in this, Now, either. It was destroyed in a great civil war long before the, Now, that we're presently in. So we'll leave that revelation for someone else to unearth. Our destiny is not to change things but just to guide them. It's a fine line we tread. It's a process I'm beginning to understand, but there's still much for me to learn. And we'll be learning much more about the wonders of life together than we could possibly have imagined. I'm sure in this, Now, many things will astound you. Try to appreciate everything around you without staring and showing too much surprise. After all, we wouldn't want to draw too much attention to ourselves, would we? When we step out of this cleft, you will see vehicles that will astound you. They move very quickly without the use of horses to draw them. They are called cars. The bigger ones are buses and the ones used to carry goods are called trucks. This day's major currency is printed on paper, and coins are used for lesser amounts. Check your pockets for money. The paper bills will probably be in a wallet."

"Yes, I've found some. Can we exchange it for food and shelter?"

"That we can, and travel, so let's go find ourselves a bus to Bristol."

It proved to be a challenging climb down to the road below. Time had washed away that part of the gorge floor, leaving the cleft higher up the cliff face, making it even more isolated than it had previously been. Walking to the street below, they could pass unnoticed from the path they had taken. With many empty buses occupying it, a car park gave ampul cover from prying eyes.

"So many people, where did they all come from? And shops, so many shops. I've never seen the likes of such a place. Even the market in Petra was not like this. It paled in comparison."

"Would you like to stop here for a while and see how the place has changed?"

"Which way are we going from here?"

"I think we should go towards Cheddar. We'll probably be able to make travel arrangements there."

"Then let us walk that way and explore as we go. I find these changes to the gorge fascinating. After all, this was my home for so many years. I lived here because I loved the isolation it provided. I was enthralled by the solitude and the wildness of the place. It was a place to study nature, a place to think. It is quite a different place today. I wonder what it will be like in another sixteen hundred years. Perhaps we will visit that, Now, one day."

"I'm glad you accept change so easily. This will be your first experience of a cultural shock of this magnitude. Perhaps we should browse the stores you'll learn a lot by seeing all the different items available for sale. There's also lots of useless trash for sale, but the materials these items are made from will amaze you. So, remember what I told you don't look surprised and don't stare." After an hour of store browsing, Merlin was board and ready to leave like most men.

On the other hand, Ruth was approximately twenty-five years beyond her, Now of origin and still fascinated by this period. The Now, she'd said goodbye to on that mountain when she bid farewell to her former life for good. The changes made in that short space of time fascinated her. Only after Merlin's insistence they leave to find a bus bound for Bristol did they depart to Gorge. The bus trip, although uneventful, captivated Merlin's imagination.

"This mode of transportation seems very efficient and very fast. It must have taken many, many men years to construct such a road as this. Are there other roads like this one?" Ruth smiled.

"This must seem very strange to you, but the road system is extensive and complex. Large machines are used in their construction and maintenance. They can do the work of hundreds of men."

"Again, where did all the people come from? Were they all born in this place? It seems inconceivable so many people can live off the land, but there does seem to be an abundance of food."

"When you consider how the population has grown over time, it then becomes easy to understand. Farming has become so efficient that it provides an adequate supply of produce for many people enabling them to multiply without the constant threat of starvation. Disease amongst the population has also been controlled more effectively than in your, Now, of origin."

"I see, all this seems so strange, but I am already accepting these changes and appreciating them. These comfortable chairs on this bus are much more relaxing than travelling by horseback. Yes, I can appreciate this form of travel."

"The chairs on a bus are referred to as seats."

"I will endeavour to remember that."

* * * * * * * *

"It looks like we're pulling into the bus station. This is where we'll be disembarking. We'll have to find lodgings for the night. I have five twenties left. How much do you have?"

"What are five twenties?"

"The number of notes I have is five. The twenty stands for how many pounds each note bearing that number is worth."

"So you have one hundred. If that is correct, and I have forty, that will make one hundred and forty pounds between us. That would seem to be a lot of money. I think we will be able to live like Kings this evening."

"I don't know. The bus fare was much more than I would have thought. Let's walk this way." She pointed in the direction that a sign indicated was a place called Harbour Side. It's probably a popular area. Perhaps we'll find a hotel there." After walking for ten minutes or so, they came to a large oval roundabout with a host of interconnecting roads. "Well, this is a busy place. The middle has water fountains covering it. Just in case you're wondering what they are. This time you can stare. No one will think it strange. This must be some sort of tourist area we've arrived at."

"The buildings are so tall. Why do they not fall over?." Ruth just laughed.

"These are small. Wait until you see a skyscraper."

"What is a skyscraper?" Ruth looked around.

"There's a small one. That blue one down to the left." Merlin's jaw dropped in amazement.

"I must take a closer look." He quickly took off in the direction of the building, barely giving Ruth time to think before following him. He stood outside and looked upwards. "It is so high. How does one reach the top?"

"Where in luck it's a hotel. Perhaps we can stay the night here if we have enough money." They went inside and up to the front desk. Ruth did the talking. "Do you have rooms available, if so? How much for the night? The young lady at the reception desk answered after checking her computer.

"We have just one room left; it's on the fourteenth floor. It's one hundred and forty pounds per night." Ruth whispered to Merlin.

"I think we should take it. I have a feeling we're supposed to be here." Merlin got his wallet out to pass his forty pounds to Ruth. At that point, the clerk interrupted.

"And will that be on your credit card, sir?" Ruth saw the card in the wallet simultaneously, as did the clerk.

"Yes, let's put it on your card, Merlin." She took it from the wallet and passed it to the clerk, who then ran it through the reader and gave the hand-set to Merlin. "There you go, sir." He gave Ruth a bewildered look.

"Men, they're hopeless; give it to me. Your key number is what's needed; you've forgotten it again, haven't you. Good grief, man. He'd forget his head if it wasn't attached." He was still looking bewildered as Ruth punched in the only number she thought it possibly could be. His gate number was accepted. The desk clerk handed them two room-door key cards and pointed them in the direction of the elevators. As the door opened, Ruth stepped in. Merlin followed.

This is a tiny room, Ruth. How can we stay the night in such a small place?" She could not control her laughter as she punched in the fourteenth floor. As it started upwards, Merlin grabbed at the walls. "What is happening? The room is moving."

"I'm so sorry I should have warned you. This elevator moves up and down. It'll take us to any floor we wish to go to. When we reach floor fourteen, the same numbers I touched on the key panel, the door will open, and we can step out."

"This truly is an amazing time we have visited Ruth."

"That it is Merlin, that it is." Standing at their suit's entrance door, Ruth showed Merlin how to use the key card.

"This is a grand room, Ruth. From the window, I can see the river below. We will not have too far to go to fetch water."

"There's something else you need to see." Taking him by the hand, she led him to the bathroom. "This is a tape. Turn it this way, and it allows water to flow. Turning it the opposite way stops the flow."

"Why are there two taps."

"One's for clod water, the other one is for hot water."

"How wondrous, hot and cold running water at a touch. But why is there a horse trough here?"

"Merlin, that's not a horse trough. It's a bathtub for bathing. A place to wash your body for good hygiene. It washes away body odder, cleanliness, you know. You saw me bathe in that natural basin in the cave."

"Yes, I remember, at night, an enemy would not get your sent and know your whereabouts. What a great strategy."

"Well, something like that. A person would also smell better in bed, which was my thought.

Speaking of the bed." She glanced towards it. "There's something else you should know." She put her hand down and unzipped his fly. "This is how this works. Is this also not a wondrous thing." She then zipped it up and down until he became aroused. He pushed her onto the bed and kissed her. All the passion of a worrier that had just done battle for the love of his lady was unleashed. She was more than willing to exploit this extreme flow of testosterone-fuelled passion. As they seethed up down to and fro, he entered her body and momentarily, all movement stopped. It was a time of appreciation. He kissed her softly on the lips, then slowly engaged in a rhythmic flow of affection in this horizontal dance of passion. As stimulation increased, so did enthusiasm until they were both exerting more energy than was possible to safely maintain. Euphoria now entered this equation, as oxygen-starved brains reaped the ultimate high from this shared sexual experience. As total exertion apex-ed, a simultaneous joint climax made this experience one to cherish and cling to for as long as possible. Now totally exhausted and with this emotional commitment in mind, more kissing cradled in each other's arms continued. Eventually, they surrendered to a much-needed restful sleep. It was a stunning finale to experience in this, Now. It was quickly cemented into an eternal shared memory.

The light was failing when they awoke. "Come, Merlin, I will show you the pleasures of a shared shower." Taking him by the hand, she led him to the bathroom, where their disrobed bodies again entwined before entering the flow of the shower. It soon digressed into an over-exaggeration of cleansing and pampering of each other bodies. Lovemaking in the warm rain seemed to be just another extension of this showering ritual Ruth taught Merlin to appreciate. She placed her hands against the shower wall and pushed herself towards him. In turn, he kissed the back of her neck before allowing himself the pleasure of indulging himself in those familiar inner depths of her body. As she bent lower, he accommodated her with as much of himself as he could possibly give. This was something she was craving, and his exertions were lifting her almost from her feet. Overcome by this passion, he'd worked himself into a frenzy that only ebbed after ejaculation was accomplished. After more kissing and cuddling, the shower was turned off, and they dried and dressed before supper.

The elevator stopped on the second floor. It opened up onto a sparsely occupied restaurant: They requested a table near a window from the waitress at reception. Merlin ordered the meals with some guidance from Ruth. When their appetites had been satisfied, it was decided to visit the bar on the ground floor. Ruth's striking good looks did not go unnoticed by every male drinking there as they approached the bar. She was now becoming accustomed to this type of attention. She now took it all in stride.

"I have a feeling this is another place we should be. We should order drinks. I know you like cider, but I suggest you try the lager. I think that's what I'm going to have."

"Then two lagers it will be. What are lagers?"

"It's a type of beer. You'll love it." As he ordered the drinks, Ruth perched herself on one of the many stools set in front of the bar. Well, doing so, she glanced around before focusing her attention on the outside door. "Merlin, make that three lagers, please. There's someone I know just walking in. I'd like you to meet him." She waved across at the entrance. "Joe over here." She again waved vigorously. "Joe Farmer, that is you, isn't it."

"My god, Ruth! The last time I saw you was when we said goodbye twenty-five years ago in South America. You've not changed one bit in all those years, but then you did say (my appearance will never change). Those were your exact words as I remember." This brought some very strange stares from other people in the bar who were close enough to appreciate what had been said. Ruth did not appear to be more than twenty-five or so herself. She laughed it off as a joke.

"Well, thanks a lot, Joe, that statement would make me about fifty or more at least. Now would you like to rephrase that?" He looked around and only then realized what he had shouted in this crowded place. There were so many ears that had overheard his statement. Ruth had become the center of attention in the bar. People began to stare. This suddenly became more attention than even Ruth was accustomed to.

"I said years, didn't I. Why did I say years when I meant months. I thought twenty-five months, well, two years or so, then got completely confused. I've had so much on my mind of late. This guest lecturer job at the university has been so consuming. It's demanding so much from me. It gets me a little befuddled at times. It's little wonder I'm getting confused so easily."

"Please, Joe, come join us. I have someone with me; I know you would love to meet. Joe, this is my husband, Merlin. Merlin, meet Joe Farmer, an old friend and college of mine."

"So you're the famous, Merlin. There are so many unanswered questions it would take days to relate everything I'd wish to ask. Perhaps we could find a less public place to talk." Ruth pointed out a more isolated area at a booth near the window.

"I think that table would be fine." She moved from her perch to resettle at the table. The two men joined her.

"You once told me you might be able to give me the location of Excalibur. Is that now possible?"

"I need a pen and paper, Joe." She took the notepad and pen from him and drew a map of the gorge. "Excalibur should still be in this location. It's buried point first straight down about two feet under the topsoil, so good luck with the hunt, Joe." Joe turned his attention to Merlin.

"What do you know of the battle of Camlann, Arthur's last battle? Were you there? If so, where is Camlann? Its location has been lost to time." Again Ruth obliged by drawing a crude map. Camlann hill, where the battle was fought, was a distinctive landscape feature. This made it easy to pinpoint its exact location. Although, over time, names had changed. Joe was utterly intrigued by Merlin's accurate account of the battle and the politics that had brought this era to an end. He took notes of every detail. "I can never tell how I came by this information. Who would believe me anyway, but it will be invaluable for my research and, hopefully, a complete survey of the site one day. Another nagging question where is Camelot? Merlin lifted his palms upwards and swung them around.

"We are here, Joe. This very place is close to where Camelot once stood."

"Tomorrow, you must show me where its walls once stood. I know places change. Familiar features are obliterated by time, but even an approximate location would give me something to work with as an archaeologist." He looked at his watch. "Time's past so quickly this evening. It's been a long day for me. I'm not as young as I used to be. Perhaps we can meet at breakfast tomorrow, say nineish, in the restaurant. We can continue with this at that time." Ruth replied.

"That's our reason for being here, Joe. So, until tomorrow then."

CHAPTER 19

J oe showed up for breakfast with a level of enthusiasm rarely seen in such a seasoned scholar. However, he could document a credible theory regarding this extraordinary legend; his thesis would be the crowning glory to an already distinguished career. If he could produce an artifact that would inequitably support his theory on the subject, this would prove to be the icing on that cake. Achieving this objective without divulging the actual source of his knowledge might prove difficult. As he joined them at the table, he was understandably in a highly emotional state. Bubbling over with excitement, he even forgot the niceties of an initial greeting. He took a seat at the table and continued the previous night's conversation without breaking stride.

"We must purchase a map of the city as soon as possible. By tracing the course of the river Avon, we should be able to establish where the castle originally stood."

"There were two rivers, Joe, although one seems to have vanished."

"Oh yes, I think I can answer that one, Merlin. The river Frome has been paved over to form the city centre. In the newspaper, I recently read how they were thinking of exposing it again and making it a feature." So yes, you're absolutely correct; there are two rivers. There's a place not too far from here called Castle Park. It refers to Bristol castle, but if what you tell me is accurate, then perhaps that castle was built over the foundations of Camelot. We must go there now." Ruth looked at Joe and smiled.

"Joe, you haven't ordered breakfast yet."

"A coffee to go will be good for me. Come, come, I'm too excited to sit here." He hustled them down to the lobby and onto the street. "This way." After walking for five minutes, they passed an ancient gateway that incorporated an equally old church built into the old wall's top.

"This place has a familiarity to it, yet I do not recognize any of the surroundings. Do you know of this place, Joe?" Joe looked at his city map.

"According to the map, it's called st John's Arch, and that church is st John's on the wall. Apparently, this guidebook's info states: It to be the old castle's main gate on the road leading north. It's one of the few portions of Bristol castle still standing. Apparently, when Oliver Cromwell sacked the castle, it's said he spared this portion of the wall. It's believed he did this because the church was built into it."

"If this is so, the river Frome should lay somewhere beneath our feet. We're standing on the outside of that wall right at this very moment. This must be the area where the old trade road to the north would have exited in Camelot castle also."

"This is possibly true. As I mentioned before, the Frome river has been paved over."

"Then we must travel south from here to reach the main gate." Walking through the arch, the road rose slightly as they walked toward Castle park and the Avon river. "This area we have entered must be within Camelot's walls." Standing near the edge of Castle Park, high above the Avon, Merlin viewed their surroundings. "Yes, this is the place at which I stood, not but a short time since." He pointed down to his left. There, the castle moat do you see. I was there when it was dug. This is the place." Ruth nodded.

"I recognize this place to Merlin. I think this is all we can do for you here, Joe."

"But wait, there is one more thing you should know, Joe. The main gate to Camelot would have been there." He pointed to an area off to their right and close to the river. Joe made a note.

"Do you have a car, Joe?" Ruth inquired.

"Yes, I have a rental." Merlin looked puzzled.

"What is a rental?"

"It's a car you borrow for a price."

"Does this price you speak of refer to payment by money. Or that strange card."

"Ether or Merlin. Joe, can you drive us to Cheddar?"

"Yes, of course, but I have no idea where Cheddar is. Although the car does have G.P.S. In it."

"That's got me foxed, Joe. What the hell is G.P.S.?"

"Oh, a lot has changed in twenty-five years, hasn't it. It kind of a built-in map that guides the way to an address."

"O.K., then let's get to that car and go."

The centre of the gorge was not so crowded as the previous day. Parking in any one of the many car parks became a matter of choice. At this moment, Joe aired his concerns about presenting his findings.

"I have no supporting evidence to the story you've told me, and I have no idea how to present it without being laughed out of town. It's so frustrating to have all this knowledge and no way to corroborate it."

Merlin was first out of the car. "Wait in this place, give me a short amount of time, and I think I can solve your dilemma." He disappeared in the cleft's direction and returned, in the time it took to reach there and back.

"It is done. Ruth, if you would be so good as to show Joe where you buried Excalibur, we can be on our way." Ruth gave Merlin an enquiring stare knowing he had been up to something. "Yes, Ruth, all will be reviled when we reach the bolder."

Hiking up through Cheddar Gorge, Ruth pointed out the rock as soon as it came into view. She started to explain to Joe where he should look, but his enthusiasm again overruled his reasoning. He ran on ahead to start his excavation. By the time they joined him at the rock, he was on his hands and knees, clearing an area near its base. "Look, writing. I think it's some kind of ancient Gaelic. This is truly amazing, more than I could have hoped for."

"It is a script which I am familiar with. Allow me, Joe." Merlin quickly related the context of the inscription. It gave an account of the battle of Camlann and an explanation of how Excalibur came to this place. Ruth again looked at Merlin, this time with a look requiring an answer. He just laughed.

"I thought it would solve Joe's dilemma if I returned to this place after I left you and wrote this text. It took a week to inscribe, and it is authentic, for it was written just days after the battle. It is a wondrous thing, the ability to move through time. When I left for that instant, I came here. In that other, Now, so long past from this, Now, I solved Joe's dilemma. I have a feeling it's time to say goodbye. Do you have that feeling also, Ruth?"

"Yes, I do." She put her arms around Joe, hugged him and kissed him on the cheek. Merlin shook him by the hand.

"What new adventure awaits the two of you?"

"I don't know the answer to that one, Joe, but I'm sure whatever it is, it will be interesting." She looked at Merlin. "How does Mt Olympus sound. I think we're supposed to be meeting the rest of the clan there. I also have this feeling there's a wedding being planned, and we're supposed to be the bride and groom."